How d
How do you
How does a..y... .u.v.v. .. ..

The monsignor reminds Jacob of the old Obi-Wan Kenobi from the original Star Wars movie. He wears dark robes like a Jedi and sits very still behind his desk, a piece of paper in his hand that Jacob suspects came from his own file.

Without looking up from the sheet of paper, the monsignor says, "Have a seat, Mr. Smithson." His voice is raspy and old, and he wheezes like Darth Vader after every couple words.

Jacob sinks into a plush leather chair facing the monsignor's desk and holds his breath.

"Sister Mary Margaret," the monsignor intones as he breathes in—more Sith than Jedi, Jacob thinks.

The nun steps forward. It's the same sister who dragged him from the cafeteria. She doesn't look at Jacob, either. Here in this office with its dark paneled walls and thick dark carpet, Jacob has ceased to exist.

Another breath. I am your father, Jacob thinks. He covers his mouth with one hand to hide his smile, but the monsignor notices. "Do you find this funny, young sir?"

Jacob snickers. "No."

The monsignor looks at Jacob for the first time, ducking his head so he can peer over the top of his wire-frame glasses.

Jacob bites the insides of his cheeks to keep from grinning.

GLBT YA Books from Prizm

Banshee by Hayden Thorne
Changing Jamie by Dakota Chase
City/Country by Nicky Gray
Comfort Me by Louis Flint Ceci
Heart Sense by KL Richardsson
Heart Song by KL Richardsson
I Kiss Girls by Gina Harris
Icarus in Flight by Hayden Thorne
Josef Jaeger by Jere' M. Fishback
Masks: Evolution by Hayden Thorne
Masks: Ordinary Champions by Hayden Thorne
Masks: Rise of Heroes by Hayden Thorne
The Mediocre Assassin's Handbook by Tamara Sheehan
Staged Life by Lija O'Brien
The Suicide Year by Lena Prodan
The Tenth Man by Tamara Sheehan
The Water Seekers by Michelle Rode
Without Sin by J. Tomas

J. Tomas

Without Sin
J. Tomas

Illustrations by Rose Lenoir

Prizm Books
a subsidiary of Torquere Press, Inc.

Without Sin

This is a work of fiction. Names, characters, places, and incidents either are the product of the author's imagination or are used fictitiously. Any resemblance to actual events, locales, organizations, or persons, living or dead, is entirely coincidental and beyond the intent of either the author or the publisher.

Without Sin
PRIZM
An imprint of Torquere Press, Inc.
PO Box 2545
Round Rock, TX 78680
Copyright 2008 © by J. Tomas
Cover illustration by Rose Lenoir
Published with permission
ISBN: 978-1-60370-684-1, 1-60370-684-4
www.prizmbooks.com
www.torquerepress.com

First Prizm Printing: April 2009
Printed in the USA

there's room under the rainbow
www.prizmbooks.com

J. Tomas

Without Sin
J. Tomas

Illustrations by Rose Lenoir

5

Without Sin

Part 1

Chapter 1

The first time Jacob Smithson notices Avery Dendritch is at morning mass on the Wednesday that classes start at St. Thomas Aquinas Catholic Boarding School for Boys.

Jacob sits with the rest of the sophomore class in the middle of a church that's filled with pew upon pew of clean-cut boys in ironed khakis and navy blazers. He's on the end of his pew and beside him is Mike Nelson, whom he already suspects he may not like. But Mike's his roommate and the only person in the whole school Jacob knows, which is one more than Sunday evening, when his dad helped him move into his dorm. Mike laughs too loud and talks too fast, but Jacob can't figure out if that's because he's nervous or just lonely, and he doesn't much care, either.

When Mike whispers something to him about a study group this evening, Jacob leans out into the aisle and pretends to concentrate on the mass. Study groups? He rolls his eyes. He hasn't even been to class yet.

Up on the altar, the priest holds the communion wafer in his hands, his eyes closed. Between the altar and Jacob's pew sit the juniors and seniors, who have learned by this stage of the game to keep their heads down and their hands folded in their laps as if in prayer, but Jacob wonders how many of them are really praying and how many can't wait for the mass to end.

He himself is one of the latter—in fact, he can't wait for this whole school year to finish. He hopes that one year is enough penance to atone for whatever he did to piss his parents off enough to finally make good on their threat of boarding school. He tells himself he doesn't know what the final straw could have been, but he knows it doesn't matter. He is just too much trouble.

"Unruly," the therapist had told his mom. "He's brilliant, Sarah, and that's part of his problem. The public school isn't structured enough for him. It's not engaging enough."

So boarding school it is, even though he isn't Catholic and this is the first mass to which he's ever been. Already he feels like a puppet on a string, jerked to his feet when the congregation rises, let loose to fall into the pew when everyone else sits.

Beside the priest stands an altar boy roughly Jacob's own age, dressed in a white cassock that hides his school uniform. He's cute, with strawberry blond hair that stands up as if a cow licked his forehead, but Jacob thinks that's the way he styled it. A quick tug of a comb when he stepped out of the shower this morning, probably running late... The thought makes Jacob nervous in a delicious way he can't quite put into words. It's the image of the altar boy in the shower that does it for him, and he covers his mouth with his hand to hide a sudden grin.

The altar boy stands with a huge book in both hands, holding it open while the priest reads from its pages. Jacob thinks it might be the Bible, but he's not sure. Earlier there were readings from the book, and they were from the Bible, so it must be a Catholic version. He leans forward and rests his chin on the pew in front of him, watching the altar boy. He likes the way the candlelight catches in those reddish blond spikes, and he wonders what the boy's name is. He wonders if the boy's a sophomore, like himself, and why he couldn't have someone like that for a roommate and not Mike, who can't sit still. Every time he shifts, Jacob hears his song sheet crinkle, and he's about ready to grab that damn piece of paper from Mike and smack him in the head with it. He doesn't care if they are in a church—Mike is one of those guys who begs to be hit.

Which is partly why I'm here, Jacob reminds himself, his gaze never leaving the altar boy. He likes the way that cassock pulls against the round butt hidden beneath the white cloth.

He used to fight in public school because he has a temper and he can't keep it in check. The teachers never understand it—he gets good grades but he can't stop fighting in the halls. His parents think this school will be different.

He has his doubts.

The priest says something that Jacob misses but around him, students surge to their feet and he lets himself be dragged along like a boat tossed in a storm. He thinks he should sit down again and see if he can start a wave, and the thought makes him giggle, but he doesn't think that would be a good idea. Not on the first day of classes.

Mike takes Jacob's hand in his and for a moment Jacob shakes free, his brow already darkening with anger. "What the—" he starts, but catches himself in time. A few of the kids in front of him turn around, bemused.

"The Our Father," Mike tells him in a loud stage whisper. He takes Jacob's hand again, and because everyone else is holding hands, Jacob doesn't pull away this time. "You hold hands for this part."

"Jesus," Jacob whispers as he lets Mike push him out into the aisle. The boy across from him is waiting, hand outstretched, and Jacob glares at it before he takes it in his own. He's all for holding hands with boys, don't get him wrong, but these dudes just aren't his type.

In front of him the aisle is filled with row after row of students, their hands linked as they begin the prayer. Jacob cranes his neck to catch a glimpse of the altar boy, so he's the only one whose head isn't bowed.

But neither is the altar boy's. He's looking around with an expression on his face that reads 'anywhere but here,' and Jacob knows that feeling all too well. When the prayer ends and everyone shuffles back to their seats, Jacob stands in the aisle a moment longer, willing the altar boy to notice him.

He does.

When he looks at Jacob, he raises his eyebrows in a wide-eyed, staring way that makes Jacob grin again. It's one of those 'why me?' looks Jacob can appreciate because, right now, he's feeling the same way.

During communion, Jacob waits his turn in the long line of boys, hands folded beneath his chin. At the altar he takes the wafer in one hand and pops it in his mouth, where it promptly sticks to his tongue. He side-steps away from the priest and makes the sign of the cross because he saw Mike do it. Forehead, he thinks, his hands following the words. Chest, left shoulder, right shoulder, chest. Amen.

He looks up and sees the altar boy watching him. With a wink, Jacob flashes him his best smile. He knows it's irresistible.

The altar boy smiles back and ducks his head shyly. But on his way back to his seat, Jacob glances over his shoulder and sees he's still being watched. He likes that.

Mike doesn't remember what the altar boy looked like. "Light red hair," Jacob tells him. "Almost blond. Sticks up in the front?"

"Do you know how many boys fit that description?" Mike sits at his desk, leaning over his geometry book. "You and me both."

"My hair's more brown than blond," Jacob tells him. "Come on, think. Pale green eyes. On the altar, damn it."

How could he not remember? Jacob can't forget. He's lying on his bed, staring at the ceiling and still thinking about that altar boy at mass. Homework is the last thing on his mind right now. "It was just this morning, Mike. How the hell do you make it through your classes with a memory as bad as yours?"

Ignoring that, Mike tells him, "I've got a schedule." He's an usher sometimes and he has a list of who serves for the month. As he looks through his notebooks for the piece of paper, Jacob asks him what he does as an usher. "Those guys who stand by the pew at communion?"

Jacob continues to stare at the ceiling; it takes him

a moment to realize Mike's waiting for an answer. "Yeah?"

"That's an usher," Mike says. "They tell you where to go when it's your turn."

"Up to the altar," Jacob says. Everyone knows that. Hell, he knows it and he's not even Catholic.

But Mike has found the paper and he holds it up as he scans it, looking for today's date. Jacob's about to snatch it from his hands when he finally says, "Avery Dendritch. Oh, him. I remember now." He puts the paper away before Jacob can ask to see it. "Why do you want to know?"

"You know him?" Jacob sits up, interested. "Is he a sophomore?"

"Avery?" Mike laughs.

He was at St. Thomas Aquinas last year and acts like he knows everyone. There are only a couple hundred boys in the whole school—Jacob's freshman class back home was larger than all four classes here combined—so he doesn't understand why Mike doesn't know more people, what with his big mouth. He thinks maybe it has to do with the way his roommate came in after dinner and closed the door on the noise in the hall so he could study. Study! Jacob still can't get over that one. Studying is something he saves for the week before exams and he vows not to do it a moment sooner.

"Avery is a senior," Mike says, turning back to his Geometry. "Been here all four years. He's in the choir."

Jacob wonders if he's as bored there as he looked on the altar. He can picture it, that boy in the choir. Probably has a pretty voice, too. Jacob thinks someone who looks like that would probably sing soprano, and squeal when he comes. And that thought does bad things to his stomach.

He's sixteen, but he's fooled around enough to know that most guys aren't quiet when they come. He sure isn't.

"A senior?" Jacob tries to keep his voice light, disinterested, but inside, his blood is boiling and his thoughts whirl out in all sorts of crazy directions.

He wants to know if Avery is seeing anyone. He wants to know if he likes boys the same way Jacob likes boys, and he wants to know if maybe he'd consider dating a sophomore. Maybe he'd consider dating me, Jacob thinks, and because that thought makes him flush, he frowns so Mike won't see how turned on he is. Avery is cute and Jacob's seen cute before, but there's something almost wicked in the way Avery looked so damn disinterested in church this morning, and Jacob likes wicked. He thinks maybe there's more to that altar boy than people think. He wants to be the one to find out.

But he thinks Mike may be the type to get all weird on him if he found out his roommate thought of other boys touching and kissing and loving him, so he keeps his mouth shut.

"I don't really know him," Mike says with a shrug. "He's two years older than me. I've never talked to him." Frowning, he glances over at Jacob and asks again, "Why do you want to know all this?"

"No reason." With a laugh, Jacob adds, "You haven't talked to him? Shit, Mike, you talk fifty-five miles a minute. I can't believe there's anyone here you haven't talked to yet." Mike blushes at that and turns back to his homework. At least he doesn't mention Avery again.

Jacob stares at the ceiling and remembers the curve of that boy's ass beneath his cassock. He whispers Avery's name under his breath, just to try it out. He likes the way it feels on his lips.

Chapter 2

Jacob expects to see Avery the next morning at mass. He sits in the middle of the pew, squeezed between Mike on his right and some kid from his English class on his left, and he keeps turning around to look back at the sacristy while the organist plays dreary tunes. The door to the sacristy is slightly ajar, but Jacob doesn't see Avery back there. It doesn't occur to him that today's schedule may be different from last night's until the altar boy leads the procession down the aisle, that Bible-like book in his hands held high, and it isn't Avery.

Something deflates inside his chest like a balloon, and he doesn't realize how much he's been hoping to see that boy again until he's not there. He wants to ask Mike why Avery isn't on the altar but that would be a little obvious now, wouldn't it? Just a tad. Besides, Mike doesn't know—he's just an usher, and only when his name comes up on the schedule. He doesn't even know Avery, not personally.

During mass Jacob kicks the back of the pew in front of him, restless and bored. When the upperclassman turns around and tells him to stop it or he'll break Jacob's leg, Jacob whispers, "I'll kick your ass."

So much for St. Thomas Aquinas helping him grow up a little.

He's sad that it's only the second day of classes and already he's falling into the same old shit that got him thrown out of public school in the first place.

When everyone stands for communion, Mike says, "Maybe you should stay here. You aren't Catholic." Like Jacob doesn't know this.

But he doesn't want to be the only one in his pew, and yesterday he discovered the wine wasn't grape juice like in the churches back home, but was real, honest-to-God wine, and he wants another sip. Yesterday he almost dropped the goblet when he drank from it, shocked to find it contained alcohol, and a heady red wine at that. He gulped it down and the swallow he took was gone before he knew it, though the taste lingered in the back of his throat all day long, the same way the memory of Avery's eyes lingered in the back of his mind.

Today he's going to drink deep and savor the wine. He's only sixteen and it's the first real drink he's ever had. So he tells Mike to shut up and folds his hands as if in prayer as he follows the boy from his English class up to the altar. He thinks about skipping the bread part—it's a thin, round wafer that sticks to his tongue like plastic and he doesn't like it all that much—but he thinks maybe someone will say something if he just jumps ahead to the wine, so he stays in place. When he gets the goblet he takes a quick sip to make sure it's still wine and it is, so he takes another sip. He'd drink the whole cup but the server takes it away. He's an upperclassman who frowns at Jacob like he's done something wrong, but Jacob simply grins and falls back into step with the other sophomores.

Jacob's head is down as he walks back to his pew, so

he sees the loafer-clad foot when it juts out into the side aisle to trip him up. He's wondering where Avery is and if he'll ever see the altar boy again. He's wishing the boy would serve every day just so he can stare at the altar— Avery has grown cuter the more Jacob thinks of the boy, so by now Avery is almost an Adonis in his mind. Jacob thinks if he ever sees Avery again, he'll swoon. Then the foot sticks out and Jacob stops an instant before he can step on it. He looks up, thinking it's that kid he got pissy with earlier, and finds himself staring into those catty eyes that haunted his dreams last night.

"Avery," he whispers, before he realizes he shouldn't say the boy's name. But Avery smiles and Jacob can't help but smile back. Was he thinking Adonis? Because that Greek god has nothing on this boy.

"Don't trip," Avery says. His voice is scales lower than Jacob imagined it would be. Then he laughs—it's a deep, throaty sound that makes Jacob ache in places he only just discovered the last few years. This time it's Avery who winks at Jacob, and there's that wicked gleam in his eyes Jacob saw the day before, that little something hinting this boy isn't as placid as everyone might think he is. "You're new here."

Jacob's about to tell Avery his name when Mike pushes against him, and Avery pulls his foot in as Jacob stumbles up the aisle. "Keep moving," Mike whispers with another shove.

If Mike touches him again, Jacob's going to kick his ass, regardless of the fact that they have to share a room together for the rest of the school year.

But Mike's not the only one pushing now, and Jacob glares at everyone who looks his way as he slides back into his pew. When the kid in his English class starts to ask him something, Jacob tells him to shut the hell up. The shocked expression on his face is enough to make Jacob feel better, but just a little. He wants to be sitting with Avery.

Several rows in front of him, Avery turns around and smiles with that hint of something more that makes Jacob want to pin him down until he confesses all the sordid thoughts going on inside his head. Jacob thinks he'd like those thoughts. There's something in Avery's eyes that suggests those thoughts mirror Jacob's own.

It's been a while since he's fooled around with a boy and he's never had a boyfriend, not like just one guy who only hung out with him and only kissed him, so his stomach flutters now and he can't pay attention to the rest of the service; he keeps looking over at Avery. He wonders if that whole foot thing can be considered flirting. He hopes so.

He leaves one of his school books beneath the pew so he'll have to go back and get it. After the mass, he leaves the church with Mike and one of Mike's friends, someone Jacob doesn't know and doesn't want to know. On the old stone steps outside, Jacob stops and makes a show of looking through his books. "I lost my history book."

Mike walks down another three steps, mouth running nonstop, but when he realizes Jacob's not coming, he stops and looks back. "What?"

"My history book," Jacob explains. "I think I left it inside. You go on—"

"We can wait," Mike says.

But Jacob shakes his head. "It's okay. I'll catch up."

Please, he prays. He doesn't want to be stuck with his roommate all the time, and he's thinking maybe he can find Avery inside the church. He's been watching the students pass him and he hasn't seen the boy yet. "Go on, Mike. It might even be back at the room. I'll see you later."

Before Mike can argue, he turns and ducks back into the church, blinking in the cool darkness. Most of the students have left already, and those who mill around the vestibule talk in muted tones that remind Jacob of watercolor paintings left in the rain. The thick scent of musty incense presses against him as he enters the nave.

The nave is brighter than the vestibule, with candles that cast flickering shadows across the holy water font and the huge crucifix that hangs behind the altar. Because he left the book here himself and lied to Mike about losing it, Jacob doesn't look at the golden effigy of Christ hanging on the cross. He keeps his gaze on the floor and his scuffed loafers and counts the pews up to the one where he was sitting.

His book is right where he left it, half shoved beneath the seat so no one will see it. He snatches it up and sticks it with the others in his arms, which he hugs to his chest as he hurries from the church. At the doors to the vestibule he stops and dips his hand into the holy water, which is colder than he thought it would be. He feels it bead on his forehead as he makes the sign of the cross before leaving.

In the vestibule only a few students remain, mostly upperclassmen who don't have morning classes or who work in the church before lunch. Jacob stares straight ahead to keep from looking at anyone, and he's almost made it outside when someone steps up beside him. "Hey, there."

Jacob whirls around and finds himself face to face with Avery, that wicked half-smile on the boy's lips again. Avery is only a few inches shorter than Jacob. When he looks up at Jacob, light shines deep in those crystalline eyes, making Jacob catch his breath. He's never seen eyes that pretty, ever.

"Hey, yourself," he sighs. This was the real reason he came back. He hoped Avery would still be here.

"How do you know my name?" Avery asks. Jacob feels his cheeks heat up and he shrugs. "What year are you?"

"Sophomore," Jacob whispers.

Avery takes his arm and steers him from the church. Outside Jacob blinks in the bright daylight. "Is this your first year at St. Thomas A-Queer-Ass?" Avery asks.

Jacob laughs. His whole body tingles beneath Avery's touch because neither of them have pulled away. "Yeah." They head for the main school building, walking slow as if they have all the time in the world. Even though Jacob's going to be late to class, he doesn't care.

Avery is looking at Jacob, his gaze drifting over Jacob's wavy bangs and the rest of his facial features to settle on the curve of his smile. He stares at Jacob's mouth and when he licks his lips, Jacob thinks he's going to fall into those endless eyes. "What did you do to deserve this?" Avery asks with a grin.

"Whole bunch of things," Jacob admits. Even though they're no longer in church, his voice is still low. He's afraid this might be a dream and if he talks any louder, Avery will disappear. "Mostly cut up in school. I get in a lot of fights."

"You?" Avery grins as if he doesn't believe it. His hand tightens on Jacob's arm. Jacob thinks now is a good time to start swooning. This close he sees how flawless Avery's skin is and wants to catch those full lips between his own, kiss them swollen. When Avery winks, Jacob's smile widens. "You don't look like a bad boy to me."

"You don't know how bad I can be," Jacob replies, pleased that he manages to sound coy and unaffected when his whole body is screaming for Avery's touch. "You don't even know my name."

Avery laughs. "I'm hoping you'll tell me."

They've reached the school building now, but Jacob doesn't want to go to class. He wants to run off into the woods behind the school, Avery in tow. He wants to tumble to the ground, Avery above him, the crush of their bodies so sweet it's almost painful. He has no clue how he's going to make it through the day with that thought in his head.

Avery holds the door open for him. "You gonna tell me?" he asks. "Or do I have to guess?"

Inside, the school building's as dismal as the church, and musty like old books. The hall is clogged with students and Jacob's class is on the other side of the building—he's already late so he's not going to rush. Hell, now that Avery is finally talking to him, he doesn't want to leave.

When he doesn't answer immediately, Avery's grin slips a notch. "Joseph?" he asks.

Jacob realizes he's staring. "What?"

"Bradley?" Avery asks. "I'm guessing."

Jacob laughs. "It's Jacob."

"Jacob," Avery breathes. For a moment his eyes slip closed as if he's savoring the name. Another squeeze on Jacob's arm and Avery lets it go. "Well then, Jacob." He says it like a prayer. "See you around."

As he walks away, he shoves his hands into his pockets.

Jacob watches the way Avery's khakis pull taut around his buttocks with each step he takes.

Even after Avery vanishes into the crowd, Jacob stands there, still smiling just slightly. Is he falling? He thinks he is.

Chapter 3

Y ou know he's gay," Mike says at lunch. He's talking about Avery. The way he says it makes his friends laugh, as if liking other boys is a bad thing.

Jacob glares at his roommate across the table. "You don't even know him."

Jacob's voice holds that undercurrent of anger that Mike will learn about soon enough. It's the anger that got Jacob kicked out of the public high school last year, when one of the other freshman thought it would be cute to call him a fag.

That had been in the boys' locker room after P.E. The kid had spent the next hour in the nurse's office, waiting for his mom to pick him up. He'd needed five stitches across his forehead where Jacob had rammed him into one of the faucets in the showers.

Jacob had spent the rest of the day in the principal's office, listening as "Dirty Harry" explained to his parents how horrible a child he could be. His therapist had been there, too. She hadn't mentioned then that he was brilliant and bored. She had just nodded in all the right places, and when Jacob left the school, he had been told not to come back.

But Mike doesn't catch the anger in Jacob's voice, mostly because he probably doesn't know it's there. He shrugs and bites into his hamburger. "I'm just saying, rumor has it."

"He likes it up the ass," another kid says, some freshman named Trevor something or other, who's decided Mike's cool just because he's a grade older and talks a good game. Jacob doesn't know where Mike finds them, but he won't be sitting here again tomorrow.

When Trevor leans over and winks at Jacob, a stupid grin on his face like he knows Jacob will get his joke, Jacob grabs his collar and hauls him across the table.

Fear flickers in Trevor's eyes. He grapples with Jacob's hand at his neck, but Jacob has had more experience with this sort of bullshit and Trevor can't pry Jacob's fingers loose. Mike's watching with wide eyes. "Shut the fuck up," Jacob growls.

"I didn't—" Trevor chokes, but Jacob shakes him until the words dry up.

Mike looks around, suddenly scared. "Jacob," he warns.

"Take it back," Jacob tells Trevor.

When Trevor shakes his head, Jacob pulls Trevor's shirt tighter around his neck. His face is turning a deep red, almost purple, and Jacob wants to hurt him for talking about Avery. Jacob bares perfect white teeth as if he were a lion and about to bite the kid's nose off, then snarls, "I said—"

"Okay," Trevor says. "Jeez, okay, I take it back. You happy? I take it back."

From the corner of his eye, Jacob sees one of the nuns heading his way. He releases Trevor, making the kid stumble from the table. Trevor lands on the floor with a thud that had to hurt and looks up at Jacob with wounded eyes. Then his gaze shifts to Mike as if asking for help, but Mike's not looking his way. Mike's staring at his plate, ignoring them both.

"Keep your goddamn mouth shut." Jacob realizes the whole cafeteria has fallen silent. Everyone's looking at them, even the lunch ladies behind the counter. Everyone but Mike. "You say shit like that again and I'll fucking kick your ass. I'll—"

Then he feels a hand grip his arm. He looks up at the nun, a young woman hidden in the habit of her order, her eyes daring him to keep it up. He tries to pull away but can't. He remembers this all too well and, without further argument, lets the nun drag him to the monsignor's office. He suspects his parents will be called. He can't imagine this will make them happy.

There's a short bench outside the monsignor's office where the nun deposits Jacob to await punishment. He thinks about running away but where would he go? Back to his room, and as this is a boarding school, it would be a no-brainer to track him down there.

So he sits on the bench with a defiant look on his face. He glares at the students passing in the hall who sneak furtive glances at him, like they've heard about what happened in the cafeteria and they're afraid his wrath will fall on them next.

A few boys laugh when they walk by. The sound only fuels the fire still simmering inside him.

Suddenly Avery is there, pushing through the crowd to reach him, and despite the sudden euphoria that washes over him, Jacob continues to pout. He's in deep shit, he knows, and he's afraid he'll be sent home now. He's not as worried about his parents' reaction as he is about losing Avery before he even gets a chance to know the boy. If he has to go home, he'll never get to know Avery the way he wants to.

Avery plops down on the bench beside Jacob, ignoring the whispers and open stares from the other students. He's not supposed to be here, talking to someone waiting to see the monsignor. He can get in trouble, too.

Jacob's almost embarrassed by the fight and doesn't want to look at Avery so he turns away.

"You didn't have to prove it to me," Avery says with a grin. "I would've believed you were a bad boy, if you wanted me to."

"You shouldn't be here," Jacob mutters, but he's happy Avery is.

"You're a celebrity." Avery picks at the crease ironed into his pants and laughs. "There aren't many fights here. Rich kids don't know how to fight."

Jacob watches the students hurry by him. "I feel like public enemy number one." He always feels bad after he gets into trouble. So why can't he stay out of trouble?

"What happened?" Avery asks.

Jacob shrugs. Defending your honor. But he just met the boy and he's not going to say that.

"Can I tell you what I heard?"

Jacob shrugs again.

Avery takes a deep breath like he's about to start a grand story. "They say you picked some freshman up over the table and threw him to the floor. They say you could hear his spine snap in two. They say—"

"That's bullshit," Jacob mutters, but he likes the shine

in Avery's eyes as he tells the story. It sounds better than what really happened. He wishes it had gone that way.

As if uninterrupted, Avery continues. "They say it took four sisters to hold you down."

Jacob laughs. "Only one. And I went willingly enough. I know the routine."

Around them the hall starts to clear as the students rush off to class before the bell rings. Jacob wonders if Avery is worried about being late. He doesn't look like he's going to leave any time soon, and Jacob doesn't want him to go.

In a quiet voice, Avery asks, "What were you fighting about?"

You. But Jacob doesn't say that. Instead, he shrugs and mumbles, "I don't know."

He's almost relieved when the door beside them opens and a nun steps out into the hall. She frowns at Avery. "Mr. Dendritch, you're going to be late."

"Yes, ma'am," Avery says, rising. He winks at Jacob and mouths, "Be good."

Jacob laughs. It's a little late for that.

"Get up, mister," the nun says. Jacob pushes himself to his feet and follows her into the monsignor's office.

The monsignor reminds Jacob of the old Obi-Wan Kenobi from the original Star Wars movie. He wears dark robes like a Jedi and sits very still behind his desk, a piece of paper in his hand that Jacob suspects came from his own file.

Without looking up from the sheet of paper, the monsignor says, "Have a seat, Mr. Smithson." His voice is raspy and old, and he wheezes like Darth Vader after every couple words.

Jacob sinks into a plush leather chair facing the monsignor's desk and holds his breath.

"Sister Mary Margaret," the monsignor intones as he breathes in—more Sith than Jedi, Jacob thinks.

The nun steps forward. It's the same sister who dragged him from the cafeteria. She doesn't look at Jacob, either. Here in this office with its dark paneled walls and thick dark carpet, Jacob has ceased to exist.

Another breath. I am your father, Jacob thinks. He covers his mouth with one hand to hide his smile, but the monsignor notices. "Do you find this funny, young sir?"

Jacob snickers. "No."

The monsignor looks at Jacob for the first time, ducking his head so he can peer over the top of his wire-frame glasses.

Jacob bites the insides of his cheeks to keep from grinning.

"Sister Mary Margaret," the monsignor starts again, and when he's sure Jacob's not going to laugh, he turns back to the paper in his hands, "tells me that you threatened another student of ours. Is that true?"

Jacob shrugs. The monsignor glances at him. "You are quoted as saying, 'I'll kick your fucking ass', end quote." The words sound like fossils in his voice, dry and dusty, specimens whose meaning has been lost over the years. "Did you say those words, Mr. Smithson?"

"Yes." Because the monsignor appears to be waiting for something more, Jacob adds, "Your honor."

"It's 'Monsignor.'" He waits another minute, but when Jacob doesn't make the correction, he sighs. "Are you going to be a troublemaker, Mr. Smithson?"

"I don't want to be," Jacob admits. I want to stay here, he adds silently, because there's this boy I think is the bomb and I want to hook up with him, and I can't if I'm not here.

But he sure as hell doesn't say that.

Another deep Vader-esque breath, and the monsignor asks, "Why did you threaten the other student?"

Jacob pouts. "He said a friend of mine liked it up the ass."

If he's hoping to shock the monsignor, he fails.

The monsignor removes his glasses and sets them aside. Without the frames he looks all the more like Obi-Wan Kenobi, with his white beard and white hair, and the lines etched into his face.

Use the Force, Luke. Jacob wishes his brain would shut up so he won't get into any more trouble.

"Fighting of any sort is not allowed on school grounds," the monsignor tells him. Jacob nods. "Do you think we should call your parents?"

Jacob shakes his head. "No." He doesn't want to hear his mom cry over the phone.

For a long moment the monsignor watches him, those heavy-lidded eyes of his pinning Jacob in place like a captured butterfly.

Jacob's afraid to meet that gaze, so he stares at his hands, twisting in his lap. He thinks of Avery. He wonders if he can find Avery after classes are over. Jacob wants to see him again.

Finally, the monsignor sighs. "Let this be a warning to you."

Maybe it is, for most boys. Maybe it scares the fight out of them. But Jacob knows the minute he's free, he'll do it again if he has to. He's scrappy like that. He doesn't want anyone walking all over him, and he doesn't want to hear them talking bad about Avery.

But he doesn't say that. Instead, he nods and mumbles, "Yes, sir. Monsignor, sir."

He watches that piece of paper disappear into his folder, which he knows will be thick as the Bible by the time he's done at St. Thomas Aquinas.

Chapter 4

When Jacob finally returns to his room, Mike is already there, bending over his desk again as he studies. He's always studying. Jacob resents him for it.

Mike looks up as Jacob slams the door shut on the whispers in the hall. Avery is right, he is a celebrity. All day long he's felt hot stares watching him everywhere he goes. He's sick of it, and he knows it'll only get worse. It'd be nice if no one would bother him now, but he knows that won't happen. Today they're scared of him—tomorrow someone else will want to pick a fight, just to say they did.

Jacob tosses his books onto his bed. From the safety of his desk, Mike asks, "Are you okay?"

"Shut up," Jacob tells him. He's not going to talk about it.

But Mike isn't listening. "I'm sorry," he says, as if it's somehow his fault. "The whole thing this afternoon—I didn't know…"

"I'm not talking to you." Jacob glares at Mike for a moment before throwing himself down on his bed. "Don't make me hurt you."

"I just—"

Jacob yells, "Shut the fuck up!"

Mike frowns but this time, he listens.

Jacob doesn't see Avery at mass. He doesn't know why, but Avery's just not there. Jacob looks for him in the faces of each student he passes, but the boys turn away because they're still afraid he's looking to fight. None of them are Avery. Somehow he convinces himself it's all Mike's fault. He leaves after communion so he won't have to listen to his roommate apologize one more time. He's still not talking to Mike.

Jacob keeps thinking Avery will appear, but he doesn't. Throughout the day, he finds himself glancing around, hoping to see the boy. He even hears Avery in the hall, or thinks so, but when he turns around, Avery's not in the crowd.

By lunchtime, Jacob is keeping his head down and ignoring the stares. He wishes he knew where Avery was. He wants to talk to the boy again. I want to do more than just talk, he thinks, and that makes him ache, which isn't a good thing. At least tomorrow's Saturday. At least there are no classes then.

He can't imagine what he's going to do on the weekend. Monday might never come.

Jacob eats his lunch outside. Mike starts to follow him but Jacob says he wants to be alone. "Go sit with your asshole friends," he says. Mike doesn't even argue.

Outside, the September sun is bright and a little too warm. Jacob takes off his blazer and rolls up the sleeves of his shirt. Then he opens the top four buttons of the shirt, revealing the white tank top he wears underneath. He misses T-shirts and cutoff shorts and jeans. He doesn't much care for a dress code.

Spreading his jacket out behind him, he lays back and stretches his arms above his head, grasping handfuls of grass. He raises one knee, folding his arms behind his head as he closes his eyes. Red patterns on his eyelids move in time with the clouds across the sun. He doesn't want to go back inside. He wonders if he can skip the rest of his classes without being caught.

When the bell rings, he doesn't move. Maybe he can stay outside during the next lunch period, too. Maybe no one will notice.

He hears students pass him on the way to the cafeteria. A few whisper his name as they go by. He hears someone mention the fight. If he weren't so relaxed, he'd get up and teach the bastard not to talk about him. But the sun has drained his energy and he just wants to lie here for a while, like a cat soaking up the sun. His legs are hot and he wishes he had on shorts. Why couldn't the dress code include shorts?

Suddenly he feels a warm weight settle on his knee as someone sits down. He opens one eye to find Avery grinning at him, his school books on his lap. He's sitting on my knee, Jacob thinks, and the way Avery looks at him makes him giddy. "I've been watching you," Avery says by way of hello. "My class is up there…"

He points, but Jacob doesn't follow his finger. He's too busy looking at the curve of Avery's neck, which is graceful from this angle.

"I've been looking for you," Jacob tells him.

"Why?" Avery shifts on Jacob's knee and the bell rings

again. "Shouldn't you be in class?"

Jacob shrugs. "You weren't at mass."

Avery laughs at that. "The whole church thing isn't really for me," he says. "I said I was sick this morning. I didn't feel like going."

Jacob should remember that. He's sure going to church every single day will get old quick.

From somewhere behind him, Jacob hears Avery's name. Avery looks up and waves. Jacob leans back, trying to see who's calling, but he's still lying on the ground and can't see anyone. Don't go, he wants to say as Avery stands up. Stay here with me. He can still feel the pressure of Avery's weight on his knee.

Avery holds one hand out to help Jacob up. "Get to class," he says as Jacob grips his hand.

He lets Avery haul him up and doesn't let go, not at first. He likes the way Avery is looking at his open shirt. He's glad his tank top is tight. His nipples stand out beneath it like nuggets, they're so hard, and for a moment Avery stares at them. Jacob bends to pick up his jacket, letting his shirt fall open more, and he feels his pants pull flat against his ass. He hopes Avery notices that, too.

"What are you doing this weekend?" Avery asks. His deep voice gets deeper, husky, and when Jacob looks at him, he swallows quickly. "There's a party tonight, if you're interested."

Jacob shrugs. "That'd be cool," he says, hoping he doesn't sound too eager. A party. He wants to ask if they'd go together, as in a date, but he doesn't.

Avery's friend calls his name again. Jacob frowns at the guy, tall and thin with dark hair. He's leaning against an open door with an impatient look on his face. "That's

Timmy," Avery says. "Tonight, then?"

Jacob grins. "Sure." He hopes Timmy isn't going. He wants Avery all to himself.

It's not until sixth period that Jacob realizes he doesn't know where the party is. He doesn't know where to meet Avery or what to wear or even if they're going as a couple, and of the three questions, the last is the one that bothers him the most.

But Avery must be thinking the same thing, because he catches up with Jacob in the hall between classes. He's a little breathless from chasing after Jacob. Jacob has to admit he likes the flush in Avery's cheeks. It adds a rosy color to his face that makes Jacob think that might be what he looks like when he comes. That's something Jacob wants to find out.

"I forgot to tell you," Avery says, touching Jacob's arm. "Meet me outside your dorm after dinner. What building are you in?"

Jacob likes the way Avery's hand rests above his elbow. "Goodman." Third floor, 323, the bed on the left, he adds silently, but Avery didn't ask for that much information. "What time after dinner?"

Avery shrugs. "Seven?"

"Sure," Jacob says with a nod. Seven sounds good. "Where's this thing at?"

If it's on school grounds, it might not be worth going to. Jacob thinks any party these kids would throw would be like the ones he went to in elementary school, in the basement of his friend Jenny's house, her mother upstairs listening out just in case anyone should have some fun.

If it got too loud—or too quiet, and she thought the kids were fooling around in the dark—she came down, clicked on the lights, and pulled out the board games. It wouldn't be long after that Jacob would head on home. He thinks St. Thomas Aquinas boys probably learned to party from Jenny's mom herself. That scares him.

But Avery must see the concern written on Jacob's face because he laughs. His hand squeezes Jacob's arm just enough to make Jacob's heart skip a beat. "It's not far," he says, lowering his voice. "Don't worry—there'll be girls there."

"I'm not worried about that." Jacob wonders if Avery is going for the girls. Did he peg Avery wrong? He hopes not. God, he hopes not.

Avery grins. With a wink, he whispers, "I didn't think you would be."

Jacob stares into those catlike eyes and doesn't remember how to breathe. In, out, in, out, he thinks, but that makes him think of sex and the one porno he ever watched, a gay film he still fantasizes about from time to time. So he tries to think of something else, anything at all, before Avery can see himself undressed in Jacob's eyes. "What should I wear?" It's all that comes to mind.

"Anything that doesn't have the damn A-Queer-Ass crest on it." He refers to the emblem embroidered onto their jackets, right above the left breast. The way he says it makes Jacob laugh. "Jeans, T-shirt, sneaks." His grin widens into a leer as he adds, "That tank top you're wearing."

"By itself?" Jacob likes how coy he sounds. So maybe they are going together.

Avery laughs again. "Seven, outside of Goodman."

Jacob notices how he avoids the question. "How are

we getting there?" There's a curfew but on weekends it's pushed back to eleven, so they shouldn't have any trouble leaving. But students aren't supposed to have cars.

"A friend of mine," Avery tells him. Jacob swallows the jealousy that surges into his throat at the words. "The party's at his house."

"He's a student here?" Jacob asks, even though he knows better. All students live in the dorms. It helps equalize them.

Avery shakes his head. "He used to be. Graduated last year, goes to State now. He's got a place a few miles away and we keep in touch."

Your boyfriend? Jacob wants to ask. Wouldn't that be a horrible joke? He's not sure he wants to go anymore.

With a shrug, Avery says, "He's picking us up."

"He doesn't mind if I go?" Jacob asks.

To his own ears he sounds young and childish. How old is he again? Sixteen... what makes him think he can compete with this friend of Avery's? This guy in college? This guy who has a place and a car of his own and throws parties on the weekend?

Avery must see the change in Jacob's face because his smile softens and he stops in the middle of the hall. "It's not like that, Jacob. He's not like that. I mean..." He trails off, not sure how much he should say.

But Jacob gets it. He flashes Avery his most angelic grin. "Okay. Seven?"

Relief floods Avery's eyes. "Seven," he agrees, nodding. He squeezes Jacob's arm again before letting go. "I'll see you then."

Avery is looking at Jacob's mouth like he wants to kiss it but knows he can't. Jacob sticks out the tip of his tongue to lick his lips. He likes the way Avery's eyes widen at that before the boy smiles and walks away.

Chapter 5

Mike sees Jacob getting ready and wants to know where he's going. He doesn't get this whole I'm not talking to you thing at all. That bothers Jacob. What's the use of being mad at someone if they don't realize it? "A party," is all he says. He's wearing that tank top Avery commented on and a pair of baggy jeans. It feels so good to be in denim again. "You're not invited."

"I don't want to go," Mike replies, as if he has a choice. "You're wearing that?"

Avery told me to, Jacob almost says, but he's not going to talk to Mike about Avery. Instead, he glares at his roommate and asks, "What's wrong with it?"

Mike doesn't answer at first. The tank top is tight and tucked into his jeans. It covers his stomach and chest like a second skin. His arms are well muscled—he likes the way they make him look older than he really is. They bulge in all the right places. The jeans are thick and dark, hanging off his hips in a sexy manner. Only a thin braided belt holds them up. He wears gold studs in his ears that he's kept out all week long because boys at the school can't wear jewelry, and he's got a slim gold chain around his neck that falls from his collarbone to pool in the hollow of his throat. He knows he looks fine.

Apparently Mike knows it too. In the end he just shrugs and says, "You should wear something on your arms. It gets cold at night."

That's what Avery is for, Jacob thinks. To keep me warm. But instead, he tells Mike, "You sound like my mother."

"I'm just saying…"

Jacob grabs a white shirt from the closet and tugs it on. "There," he says. "You happy?"

He leaves the shirt and cuffs unbuttoned because he's had to button all his school shirts up to the neck. This shirt isn't one of those. This shirt is so thin, it's almost translucent, and his tank top shines through. Mike was right, he did need something on his arms. If only so he can be helped out of it later.

He knows there's going to be a later.

Avery is already outside his building when he comes down. "You look great," Avery says, gaze straying to Jacob's waist, where his pants hang low. Jacob resists the urge to hitch them up because he likes the way Avery stares at him.

"So do you." Avery is wearing tight jeans and a white T-shirt. A black vest covers the shirt, tied across Avery's chest with a thin cord. Jacob can't wait to untie that vest, push it aside, and get his hands and his lips on Avery. He thinks he might try to untie it with his teeth, if given the chance.

They head for the gate that surrounds the school. Avery's hands are shoved deep into his pockets. Jacob wants to hold one of them and can't, so he sticks his own hands into the back pockets of his jeans. He doesn't know what to say. "Thanks for inviting me."

"No problem." With a shy smile, Avery adds, "I didn't want to go alone."

Jacob laughs. "Can I ask you something?"

Avery nods.

"If I'm totally off the mark, let me know. Don't get all freaked out on me, okay?"

"About what?" Avery frowns at him. His step falters.

Jacob takes a deep breath. He has to know if this is going to work out. He has to know if he stands a chance… "Are we going together?" Before Avery answers, he hurries to explain. "I mean, tonight. Is this like a date?"

Please, he prays. Don't let me be wrong about you.

For a moment Avery studies him, thinking. His gaze rests on Jacob's lips again. Finally he smiles that shy grin of his. "If you want it to be." His voice is so soft, Jacob has to strain to hear it.

"I do," Jacob replies, just as softly.

Avery laughs, a deep, rich sound that makes Jacob smile. "Well," he says, relieved. "That was a little awkward."

Jacob moves closer, until his elbow brushes Avery's back. "Just a little," he admits, but he's grinning like a fool because it's a date now, isn't it? He wants it to be, so it is.

Outside the gate, Avery waves at a guy leaning against an old, beat up Chevy. The car door is open and a woman sits in the passenger seat, her long legs bare beneath a short skirt. She's got curly auburn hair that falls to her shoulders. One of the guy's hands rests high up on her thigh.

The guy is young and thin, his hair split down the middle and falling to the tops of his ears. He has a hoop in his eyebrow and a smile that looks like a heart, his lips are that perfect. "Avery!" he cries, like he hasn't seen him in years. He hugs Avery quickly and winks at Jacob. "Dude, are you even legal?"

Jacob feels his cheeks burn with anger, but Avery laughs.

"Am I?" Avery asks. Probably not. "Hell, Parker, are you? I don't think so."

"Ah, but Steve is," the guy reminds him, this Parker. Jacob doesn't ask who Steve is. "He got us two kegs, my man. Two!" To Jacob, he asks, "What's your name, kid?"

"Jacob," Avery replies. "Don't call him 'kid.'"

"My bad," Parker says quickly. Then, with a conspiratorial whisper, he says, "I hear you kicked some punk's ass for picking on my boy." He thumps Avery on the back with one heavy hand.

Jacob grins, embarrassed. He ducks his head and stares at the ground. He didn't know Avery knew why he got in that fight in the first place. And he told his friend about it. Jesus.

"What did Darth Vader say to you?" Parker wants to know. In a freaky imitation of the monsignor, he intones, "I feel a great disturbance in the Force, young Skywalker."

Jacob laughs. He likes this guy. Parker claps his shoulder as if they're old friends and opens the back door of the car. "Get in, boys," he says. "The night's young and my date's horny."

In the front seat, the woman giggles but doesn't speak. She looks a lot older than Parker.

J. Tomas

They slide into the back seat. When the car starts, Avery takes Jacob's hand in his. His grip is sure and firm, his skin warm. It's softer than Jacob imagined. His fingers entwine with Jacob's and he smiles when Jacob looks at him. "Scoot over a little," he whispers.

Jacob moves closer. Avery lets go of his hand and eases an arm around Jacob's waist. Then he takes Jacob's hand again. Jacob leans against his shoulder.

He hopes it's more than a few miles to the party. He's just getting comfortable.

When they reach the house, Parker drapes an arm around Jacob's shoulders, pulling him aside. "If anyone asks," he tells him, his voice low, "you're Marie's cousin from out of town. Senior in high school, even though you don't look it."

"Who's Marie?" Jacob thinks it might be the woman from the front seat.

He's right. Parker points to her and adds, "If we get busted, you run. I got a house full of minors drinking as it is. You hear me?"

Jacob nods. This is the first party he's ever been to with alcohol. He wonders if he'll be able to con a drink. Hadn't Parker said two kegs? Jacob's not sure what a keg is but he likes the idea of getting drunk.

Inside, the house is dark and loud. Music vibrates the walls, it's turned up so high. When Avery speaks to him, he has to put his mouth against Jacob's ear and shout. It's the only way to hear anyone. No one seems to notice, though, and Jacob doesn't mind. This close, Avery smells like Irish Spring soap and Usher cologne. "Want a drink?"

41

Jacob grins. "Sure," he calls back, but Avery has already slipped away. He looks around for someone he might know but the place is full of strangers. Even Parker is gone, and he wouldn't recognize Marie if he ran into her. Behind him, more people come into the house. He lets them push him into the living room, where the stereo blares like a caged animal and there's no room to walk. Too many people dance and grind and move against each other. Jacob dances his way into the midst of them. He likes the strangers' bodies touching his, rubbing into him.

Then it's Avery sidling up to him, two plastic cups of cold beer in hand. Jacob takes one as if he does this every weekend. He tries not to grimace at the malty taste as he gulps down a fourth of the beer. He didn't realize he was so damn thirsty.

"Thanks for bringing me," he says again.

Avery can't quite hear him so he leans closer. One arm snakes around Jacob's waist as he presses against him. "What?"

Jacob doesn't remember what he said. The music is nothing but noise, the people just jostling, annoying now that Avery is holding him. Holding him. He can't get over this.

"Jacob?" Avery laughs. His breath smells like beer and is so warm against Jacob's cheek. "What did you say?"

Jacob shakes his head. "Nothing." Don't let go, he prays.

His heart thuds in time with the rapid beat. He downs the rest of his beer without tasting it.

Chapter 6

By his third beer, the music doesn't seem so loud anymore. Faces have grown fuzzy, indistinct, as if he's lost in a dream and nothing is as it seems. He vaguely thinks they should start heading back to the school, but that thought flits through his mind and disappears. He's having too much fun to go back.

Jacob's not sure where Avery is. The kitchen, maybe, because Avery told him he would be right back, he needed a refill, and Parker's in the kitchen so the kegs have to be in there, too. Jacob would follow him but he's not sure where the kitchen is.

He's not even sure where the front door is anymore.

Without missing a beat, Jacob dances out of the crowd. He leans against the wall almost gratefully. His legs are tired, his feet hurt, his head is starting to buzz like sluggish flies in summer heat, and his stomach churns like a Ferris wheel, over and over. He thinks he might be sick. Too much. Too much drink, too much dance, just too much everything. He might want to go back now.

Leaning his head against the wall, he lets his eyes slip closed. He hopes Avery finds him soon. Avery…

A hand slips around his stomach. Jacob opens his eyes,

a smile already on his lips. But it's not Avery standing over him. It's not Avery's crystal clear eyes staring at him through the smoky haze that hangs in the room like a fog. It's someone else, with coffee-colored skin, brown eyes like chocolate, and dark hair twisted into wiry dreadlocks. Thin lips framed with the beginnings of a devilish goatee.

"Hey there," this stranger says. His voice is high and seductive. Jacob suspects this is the way the angel Lucifer talked before the fall. "What's your name, boy?"

"Jacob." The hand on his stomach slips lower to toy with the buckle of his belt. It's a warm pressure he likes, even if it isn't Avery's hand.

The guy smells like cloves and cinnamon. When he smiles, Jacob sees pointy little teeth on either side of his mouth. "Tyrone," the stranger says, introducing himself. "You a friend of Parker's?"

Tyrone's hand slips another notch. It's playing with Jacob's zipper now, and Jacob's already hard, he's been hard since he saw Avery in those tight jeans. He tries to remember his story. Is he a friend of Parker's? "Marie's cousin," he says. He thinks that's right.

Tyrone laughs. "Marie?" With a quick glance over his shoulder at the crowd, he asks, "Which one is she?"

"I don't know," Jacob admits.

With his other hand, Tyrone tugs at one of Jacob's curls. "You don't know." He grins like that's the cutest thing he's ever heard.

Jacob holds up his empty cup of beer in both hands like a shield. He wishes it were full. He wants something to drink.

Leaning his head against the wall beside Jacob's, Tyrone asks, "So you're here by yourself?"

Jacob shakes his head. "I'm with Avery," he whispers. Because he likes the sound of that, he says it again, louder. "Avery."

"Avery?" Tyrone asks. He frowns at the name. "You mean—"

"He means me."

Jacob looks past Tyrone's shoulder and sees Avery there, his light eyes shiny with drink. "Hands off, Ty. Find your own boy. This one's mine."

Tyrone's hand drops away. He steps back, suddenly apologetic. "You're from Aquinas," he says bitterly, as if Jacob lied to him. "Avery, I didn't know. I swear…"

Avery pulls Jacob close. An arm goes around Jacob's waist protectively and Jacob rests his head on Avery's shoulder. He's not feeling well. The look in Avery's eyes says 'mine,' loud and clear. Tyrone disappears into the crowd.

"Avery," Jacob moans. He wants to lie down. "Who's that?"

Avery can't hear him. "Come on," he says, leading Jacob away. Someplace quiet, that's all Jacob wants. Someplace soft and quiet, where Avery can stay with him. He came to this party to see Avery. Jacob hasn't seen much of him all night.

Avery takes him upstairs, to a little room at the end of the hall. It's dark here, not quite so noisy, and they're alone. Finally, they're alone.

As Avery closes the door, Jacob frowns. "What time is it?" His voice slurs.

Avery shrugs. "It's getting late." He helps Jacob to

the bed. "We can stay here. I don't think Parker's in any shape to drive us back."

Jacob sits on the edge of the bed and yawns. Suddenly he's very sleepy. He falls back to the mattress and closes his eyes.

The bed shifts as Avery crawls over him. "You tired?" Avery whispers, his voice purring against Jacob's neck. Warm lips leave damp imprints along his jaw and a knee rises between his legs, pressing sweetly into his crotch. Jacob's breath is a hiss in the darkness.

"Not too tired," he sighs.

Avery's lips find his. They're soft and hungry and insistent, pushing Jacob back against the bed. He tastes like beer but he's more intoxicating than anything Jacob's had to drink all night. When he breathes Jacob's name, it's like gasoline, fanning the flames that lick through Jacob, igniting them both.

A hand trails down his chest, pushing his open shirt out of the way. He moans as Avery catches his lower lip between his teeth. Avery laughs, the sound rumbling through him like thunder, and Jacob grabs Avery's vest in both hands, holding him close. "How old are you again?" Avery wants to know.

"Old enough," Jacob replies. Avery's fingers pluck at his nipples, sending shivers of delight through his body.

Avery kisses him again, and again, until they're both breathless and aching. Jacob shrugs out of his shirt and Avery kisses his biceps, his tongue licking between Jacob's lips to trail down the hard muscles. For all the fooling around he's done, Jacob's never had someone do that. He quite likes the way it feels.

And he loves the kisses. He's never made out for long before—he's always just gotten it on and gotten it over with, he's never really taken the time to make it last. But right now his whole body is on edge, he's so damn hard he can't even think anymore, he's never had anyone make him feel like this before tonight. No one before Avery. It's as if no one else exists. It's just the two of them, their moans and pants drowning out the sounds of the party downstairs, their hearts beating in time with the music below. And they still have their clothes on. This amazes him.

He thinks if they ever get past this stage, they'll both explode.

Avery holds him in the darkness, his body a welcome weight pressing against Jacob, pinning him down. With tiny kisses, Avery traces the curve of Jacob's cheek from his eyebrow to his mouth and then up the other side. It's as if his skin were honey and Avery can't get enough. When he speaks, his lips barely leave Jacob's flesh. "Have you ever had sex?"

Every time anyone's asked him this, Jacob has always said yes, but he's never done it. He talks a good game but he's never dared do it. And for once he doesn't lie about that. "No," he breathes. Easing a hand down between them, he rubs the bulge in Avery's jeans and adds, "I've been around a bit, though. Just never all the way."

He can feel Avery's smile against his neck. "Has anyone ever told you how sexy you are?"

In response, Jacob catches Avery's mouth with his and stills the questions with a kiss. He's not thinking about anyone else. Avery's lips and hands have erased every guy he's ever known. Avery is all that's left.

Jacob wakes with a headache and a cottony taste in his mouth. He grimaces as he looks around at the unfamiliar room, dimly lit by the morning sun that peeks through the closed blinds. He doesn't remember where he is.

Beside him someone draws a long, shuddery breath. Avery.

He glances over his shoulder, only to find himself in Avery's arms. Jacob looks at the shadows cast on Avery's cheeks by his eyelashes, the pale skin, the pinked lips, and it all comes back in a rush. The party. Parker. The beer. The guy who hit on him, the one Avery called Tyrone. The kisses. Avery's hands on his body, the kisses, the press of Avery's crotch against his own. How could he have forgotten that? Just thinking about it again makes him tingle.

Avery's head is buried against his back. When he rolls over, Avery's arms tighten around him, like he's an anchor and the only thing Avery holds onto. They're so close, he's breathing Avery's breath.

He kisses Avery's lips, which are softer than he remembers and just as sweet. He wonders how far they went last night. He thinks they didn't get too far, since he's still wearing his tank top and boxers, and Avery's T-shirt is warm against his palms where it stretches across the boy's shoulders.

He wonders what they are now. Friends? Not really— Jacob doesn't know much about Avery, not as much as he wants to. More than that? He hopes so. God, he hopes so.

He's waking up in Avery's arms—doesn't that say something?

The bed is so warm and Avery's arms strong around his waist. Jacob almost hates to go to the bathroom, but he has no choice. Did he only have three beers? From the pressure on his bladder, he'd swear it was more. He'd swear he drank a whole damn keg.

As carefully as he can, he extracts himself from Avery's embrace. Avery murmurs but doesn't wake. The morning air is chilly against Jacob's legs as he slips from beneath the covers. His shirt and jeans lie in a heap on the floor. Avery's jeans and that tiny black vest he wore last night are all tangled up in Jacob's clothes. He likes the way they look together, so easy, so natural.

In his boxers, he hurries down the hall to the bathroom. He wonders if they're the only ones who spent the night. He wonders what time the party broke up. Part of him thinks it's still going on inside him, because his head is pounding something fierce and when he flicks on the bathroom light, he wishes he were blind. Then he wouldn't have to see the glare reflected from the white porcelain. He doesn't even look in the mirror. He wonders how they'll get back to the school. They might get in trouble for breaking curfew. He's sure Mike told someone when he didn't come back last night.

And then there was morning mass. Fuck it, he thinks. He's been to church more times this week than he has in the past year. One mass won't hurt him. He'll say the rosary to make up for it.

That makes him laugh. He doesn't know how to say the rosary. He didn't even own a set of the prayer beads until his parents took him to a Catholic bookstore last month for school supplies, but he's never used them.

Maybe Parker will take them back to the school. Right now, though, he only wants to get back into the bed, close his eyes, and breathe deep Avery's own breath.

Chapter 7

Avery is still asleep when he gets back to the room. It's cool and dark here, a relief from the bathroom light, and Jacob slips beneath the covers again as if he never left. He snuggles up to Avery until those arms wrap around him one more time. Avery's breath is warm against his neck. He drapes a leg over Jacob's hip, his foot smoothing across Jacob's thigh. The soft pillow of his genitals rests against Jacob's butt, which makes him wonder if a few well-aimed wiggles will flare Avery's erection back to life.

But it's still early. Jacob doesn't want to ruin this moment. He's never slept with anyone before.

Some time later, he wakes to tiny kisses along the nape of his neck. Damp lips tickle the skin just above his tank top, and despite his slight hangover, he snickers breathlessly. He thinks no one should ever sleep alone. He doesn't know how he'll get up in the morning after this, with no one there beside him to kiss him awake. He thinks it'll be cold then, too cold, and right now he likes the spread of Avery's hands across his stomach, the feel of Avery's lips against his neck.

"Morning, glory," Avery purrs. His voice is rumbly

and half-awake. Jacob loves it.

As he turns in Avery's arms, Avery kisses a trail across his collarbone. Jacob's decided he quite likes being kissed. He likes this boy, who can't stop touching him, who acts as if he's the only thing in the world. Today he suspects he might be, and together they're all that matters.

"Morning yourself," he mumbles, easing his arms around Avery's neck. One hand fists into thick reddish-blond hair, pulling him down for another kiss, a real one, smack dab on the lips. Jacob can't get enough of these kisses. The best thing his parents have ever done for him is send him to this Catholic boarding school.

Avery shifts onto him—Jacob was right, just a few kisses and that pillowy cushion in his briefs hardens. It presses against Jacob's own erection with a sweet crush that's almost painful. Maybe they'll go farther now that they're both awake and very much undrunk. Jacob hopes so.

But instead, Avery slides off Jacob. He's got one arm beneath Jacob's shoulders, his fingers toying with disheveled curls. The other hand rubs across Jacob's stomach, smoothing down Jacob's shirt, spreading warmth in its wake. His knee is still across Jacob's hips, his thigh against Jacob's crotch to keep him interested. Every now and then that hand on Jacob's stomach dips lower, taunting, but it never goes below the waistband of his boxers, no matter how much Jacob wants it to.

With his head on the pillow beside Jacob's own, Avery stares at Jacob for long moments and doesn't say a word. Jacob lets his fingers explore Avery's arm, his chest, his neck. They pluck at the nipples standing beneath Avery's T-shirt. They entangle in the short cropped hair above Avery's ears. Jacob's never touched a boy like this.

Somehow it's more intimate than anything he's ever done before.

"Tell me what you like," Avery whispers.

Jacob thinks he means what turns him on. "I like this." At Avery's grin, Jacob's hand slips between them to cup the front of his friend's briefs. "And I like this."

Avery laughs. "Don't make me guess." Before Jacob can reply, Avery closes his eyes and thinks, suddenly serious. Jacob leans up and kisses his chin. That brings another smile to Avery's lips. "You're sixteen."

"Yeah." Jacob frowns. "I got held back a year. That's not a problem, is it?"

"Should it be?" Avery looks at him, expectant. Jacob shakes his head. "You're only a year younger than me. Jeez, it's not like you're twelve, you know?"

Jacob laughs at that. "You like twelve year olds?" he jokes. He likes the blush that colors Avery's cheeks. "You like them young, I bet."

"Not too young," Avery says. "But Tyrone does."

"Tyrone?" Jacob vaguely remembers hearing the name before.

"From the party?" Avery prompts. Now Jacob remembers—the guy who hit on him last night. "Guess how old he is."

Jacob can't imagine. "Twenty?" He doesn't really remember much of the guy. Everything before Avery's kisses is hazy.

"Twenty-three," Avery tells him. He pushes on Jacob's chin to close his mouth. "See? He likes them young."

"I'd say." Twenty-three. Jacob doesn't know anyone that old. He doesn't know anyone older than Avery, except maybe Parker, and he didn't even talk to Parker much. He thinks twenty-three is a magical age. When he's that old, he'll finally be able to do anything he wants. No school, no parental rules, no one to bother him. He'll have a place of his own and he'll party every night, not just on the weekends. He hopes he will still know Avery then.

Avery's hand trails down Jacob's chest and back to his stomach, where the tank top has pulled up a little, exposing his bare midriff. Avery traces lazy circles around his belly button. "Tell me about yourself." Avery punctuates each word with a kiss to Jacob's temple.

So Jacob tells him about his mother and father, and how he always manages to disappoint them both. He tells Avery about his therapist, the one from the public high school who thinks he's brilliant. He tells Avery about the principal there who thinks he's trouble. He talks about his little brother, only five and already so enamored with his older sibling that Jacob can do no wrong in his eyes. The last time Jacob spoke to his mom, she told him Johnny even has Jacob's mouth, and she's glad he's away at school because she thinks maybe the kid will grow out of it. She hopes it's just a stage he's going through. She no longer thinks Jacob's is.

Avery watches him closely as he talks. Jacob feels self-conscious at first, so he ducks his head and doesn't meet Avery's frank gaze. But their legs are still tangled together beneath the sheets, Avery's hands are still on his stomach and hair, and Jacob still touches Avery with gentle, inquisitive fingers. Avery doesn't pull away. Every now and then Avery leans over and kisses Jacob's neck, just to reassure him. When Jacob realizes Avery's not going anywhere, he nuzzles closer until Avery's chin rests on top of his head. He has discovered he loves being held like this.

Finally, having run out of things to say, Jacob falls quiet. He wants to ask Avery to tell him about his own family, where they live, what Avery plans to do after leaving St. Thomas Aquinas, but he doesn't. Avery's breathing is even and slow, and Jacob thinks the boy might have fallen back asleep. He wouldn't blame Avery if he had, Jacob's life is pretty boring. "Avery?" His voice is almost a whisper.

In response, Avery kisses his forehead. "We should get back."

"Will we get in trouble, do you think?" Jacob asks. He means for missing curfew.

But Avery shakes his head. "Who'll know?"

Mike. If there's anyone who would resent Jacob for having a good time, it would be his roommate, he's sure. He probably called the monsignor at 11:01 last night when Jacob didn't come through the door.

"If anyone asks," Avery tells him, "you spent the night at a friend's. Hell, no one knows we weren't in the dorms. We just weren't in our rooms."

"True." Jacob likes the fact that they aren't at the dorms right now. He likes being in a strange bed with Avery beside him. He likes being off school grounds. It makes him feel grown-up and free in a way that spending the night at a friend's house back home never could. He thinks when he's twenty-three and living in a place of his own, he'd like to do this, spend the night in rooms he's not used to and wake up in the arms of a lover. Though he could do without the faint headache that still haunts him. By twenty-three he should be able to hold his beer.

Now Avery sits up, letting the sheets fall away, and he grins down at Jacob. "Come on then."

A sudden fear grips Jacob's heart. He doesn't want to

leave this room, this bed, these arms, not without some promise that this won't fade. He wants to be sure he'll be this safe, this comfortable, again. But he doesn't want to say anything and scare Avery away. He's not even sure what it is he wants to say…

I like you. That might work. I think I could fall for you, Avery. I know I'm only sixteen and it was only one night, but I really like you and I don't want to go back to the school if it means we'll lose whatever it is that's come between us now. I don't want to lose that, ever. I don't want to lose you.

Maybe Avery sees that in Jacob's face because he stops and kisses Jacob tenderly.

"I don't want to go back right yet," Jacob whispers.

Avery grins. "Jacob," he starts, and then he shakes his head. "I don't usually sleep with someone on the first date."

Jacob laughs.

Whatever tension stretched between them disperses as if it were never even there. "I like you," Avery says. "I want to see you again—"

"You will," Jacob promises. "I like you, too. A lot."

He sees that wicked gleam in Avery's eyes, the one he noticed the first time he saw the boy, and he laughs again. "Just don't tell anyone about this," he teases as Avery climbs out of bed. "I don't want to ruin my reputation."

That makes Avery laugh. "You do that well enough yourself."

Jacob tackles Avery and they both fall back to the bed. Now he's on top, and he grinds his hips into Avery's. It doesn't take much to make him horny all over again. "Hush up," he admonishes. He kisses the tip of Avery's nose. "I was defending your honor."

"Be careful," Avery tells him, serious again. "I don't want you sent home, you hear me? They'll kick you out of school for fighting."

"I know that." Jacob does know it. He doesn't want to be sent home.

"We can't be together if you're expelled." Avery catches Jacob's face in both of his hands. His palms are warm against Jacob's cheeks. "You hear me? No more fights."

"I hear you," Jacob says, but what he heard was we can't be together if. He heard that if. "Does this mean we're together now?"

With another kiss, Avery says, "If you want us to be."

He does. Oh, God, he does.

Chapter 8

Jacob dresses quickly. He feels as rumpled as his jeans. His shirt smells like sour beer and cigarette smoke, so he doesn't put it on. Instead, he ties it around his waist, over his belt, and tucks his tank top into his jeans. He'd like to shower but he'd have to put on the same clothes and he doesn't want to do that, not if he cleans up. He'll wait until they get back to the school. Then he'll shower and fall into bed. He thinks he can sleep until this evening with no problem, he's that tired. Well, not so much tired as his head still hurts, just enough to make him want to lie down again. Upstairs, he thinks, following Avery down the steps to the living room. I want to lie back down upstairs with him again. He wishes he were twenty-three now. He wishes he lived here and woke up beside Avery every morning.

Parker's asleep on the couch, snoring softly. Jacob thinks he probably passed out there—he's still fully dressed and looks like a rag doll just tossed aside. A small pretzel is stuck to one cheek, and as they tiptoe by the couch, Jacob reaches out and flicks the pretzel away. Parker snorts and raises a hand to rub his cheek but he doesn't wake.

When his hand falls back to the couch, the outline of the pretzel is still on his face, like a ghost pressed into his skin. Jacob thinks Parker would be a fun guy to know.

Marie offers to take them back to the school. The car keys are in Parker's pocket. Marie rolls him onto his side and sticks her hand in the pocket, grabs the keys, then rolls him back. Jacob wonders how close they are, Parker and Marie. There's only a thin piece of fabric between a pocket and skin, and Jacob knows all too well what he can feel if he sticks his hand in his own pockets deep enough. He wants to dig into Avery's pockets, just to touch bottom and see what he can find.

Avery is looking at him as if he hears Jacob's thoughts.

Remembering the way they rubbed against each other last night, Jacob blushes and grins at him. Jacob hopes they get a chance to do that again. Didn't he ask if Jacob had ever had sex? So maybe that means he wants to have sex with Jacob, and that thought makes Jacob anxious. He's only sixteen but other guys his age are doing it, aren't they?

Don't rush it, Jacob warns himself as they follow Marie outside to the car. Right now he just wants more kisses, and to be held again, and maybe that will lead to more. He hopes so.

Marie unlocks the passenger side door for them. "You two can squeeze in here," she says. "It'll look stupid if you're in the back, like I'm your chauffeur or something."

Jacob frowns at the bucket seat. He's noticed Marie says or something a lot, like she gets tired of talking and just uses it as a cop out to indicate everything else she wants to say. Somehow he doesn't think they'll both fit in the front together. "I can sit in the back," he says, a little dubious. Marie's already on the other side of the car, sliding behind the wheel.

"I want you to sit with me." Avery gets in but the seat isn't as big as it looks—when he scoots over toward Marie, the gear shaft sticks in his side.

"It's okay." Jacob would rather they both sat in the back, but if he has to, he thinks maybe he can manage it alone. If he has to.

But Avery shakes his head. Scooting back onto the seat, he pats his lap. "Sit down."

Jacob smirks. Marie laughs as he climbs into the car and sits on Avery's knees. He holds the dashboard with one hand as Avery slams the door shut. It's not too bad. At least they're together…

Avery grabs his waist and pulls him back until he's pressed against Avery. Then he clamps the seat belt in place, buckling them both into the seat. When Avery spreads his legs, Jacob falls to the seat, his butt tight in the V of Avery's crotch. He knows that's not the gear shaft poking into him.

He stares out the window beside him as Avery tells Marie how to get back to the school. Avery's hands are laced low across his waist, a sweet pressure against his groin. He doesn't want to go back to St. Thomas Aquinas right now. He wants to ask Marie to keep driving, past the turnoff, just to see where the road takes them. Mike's waiting for him back at the dorm, and he's sure there will be whispers and stares. As if the kids don't talk about him enough already. Someone must have seen the two of them leave yesterday.

He's not too worried about that, really—he can hold his own in a fight, and he knows most kids don't expect that. They'll call him "fairy" and "faggot" and think he'll let them get away with it, like that kid in the cafeteria. Well, that hadn't been about him, but the kid talked shit about Avery and he won't put up with that, either. That's my boy you're talking about, he thinks. He likes the sound of that.

But he doesn't want to fight. Fighting means he'll get in trouble. Trouble means one of the nuns will haul his ass into the monsignor's office, and Darth Vader will call his parents the next time, he knows it. They always give him one warning, a Get Out of Jail Free card, and it's never enough. He's always blown it before. First the warning. Then the phone call. His mom will cry and his father will want to know what it's all about this time, and he can't tell them because they don't know he likes boys. They don't know other kids hate him because he doesn't get hard on girls.

After the phone call, he gets sent home. That's the way it's always worked at public school. Only this time, he doesn't want to go home. He's finally found a boy he likes, a boy who likes him back. Someone who's more than just groping hands in the back of a movie theater, a quick handjob in the bathroom between classes, a blowjob in the woods behind his house. Once or twice and Jacob never saw those boys again. It was always someone different, someone who heard Jacob liked to do that and was a little curious about it, and because he does like to do it, he did. But he hasn't in a while now. Most of the kids back home are scared of him. He gets into too much trouble.

For all the fooling around he's done, he's never fooled himself that it was more than just the moment. He likes to get off so he finds a boy to get off with. But now here's a boy holding him who didn't get off last night, neither of them did, and he's still here. His arms are around Jacob's waist. His fingers are entwined with Jacob's. He's laughing at something Marie's said that Jacob didn't hear. Jacob can feel that laughter rumble through Avery's chest.

He wants to get Avery alone again. He's never wanted any boy so bad.

Marie lets them out at the gate. The buildings of St. Thomas Aquinas are back off the road, and rolling green hills stretch between the gatehouse and the church. The dorms and school building aren't even visible from the car. They watch her drive off, then head for the school. Dread curls in Jacob's stomach as they near the gatehouse, but the uniformed guard doesn't even look up from his paper when they pass by.

"See?" Avery whispers. Around them, the school is quiet. They could be the only ones awake at this hour, even though it's almost ten in the morning, but Jacob knows they're not. Everyone else is probably in mass. "I told you not to worry."

Jacob laughs at that. He shoves his hands into his pockets because he wants to touch Avery again and can't. Or rather, shouldn't. He doesn't know who's watching.

Outside Jacob's building, Avery stands so close to him, their hips bump. Jacob can feel Avery's hand through his pocket. Avery rubs Jacob's wrist and stares at the gold necklace that winks at Jacob's throat. "I had a good time," Avery murmurs.

"Me too." Jacob squints as he looks at the church, wondering if Mike is inside, if his room is empty. He doesn't know, but he doesn't want to chance it so he doesn't ask Avery to come up. Without looking at Avery, he says softly, "I want another kiss."

Avery laughs. "Me too."

With a wry grin, Jacob sighs. "No goodbye kiss." He doesn't like that. He can count the number of real dates he's had on one hand and each one of them ended with a kiss. Not just a peck, either, but something long and drawn out and breathless. Something that left him aching and made him want more.

"I would but…" Avery shrugs.

He doesn't have to say it—Jacob knows. They have to be careful. Would the monsignor throw them out for kissing? Probably. The nuns would be in an uproar, two boys getting it on. And God, that is so not the way he wants his parents to find out.

Smiling slightly, Avery adds, "This isn't goodbye. I'm going to see you again."

He doesn't ask. He says it as if he knows it's the truth, and Jacob loves that.

Jacob feels like a fool when he grins back. "Tonight?" he asks, hopeful.

Avery nods. "We have mass tonight."

Shit. School rules state that a student can only miss one mass a week without written permission by the staff, and no more than three masses a month. Weekdays the mass is in the morning, before classes start, but Saturdays and Sundays there are two services, one at quarter to 9:00 in the morning, the other at 6:30 in the evening for those who oversleep. They missed the early service today. Jacob doesn't really want to go tonight. "We can skip it," he suggests.

Avery touches his wrist again, his finger soft like spider

webs. "We can go together," he says. "They don't make you sit with your class on the weekends."

"Really?" Jacob imagines sitting beside Avery on the hard wooden pew, their knees touching, holding hands during the Our Father.

Avery nods again. As if searching for something more to say, he asks, "You going back to sleep?"

Jacob knows they're only talking so they don't have to part. He doesn't want Avery to leave just yet. "I think so," he says. "After a shower. I stink."

Avery sighs in a lovelorn way that makes Jacob's heart flutter. "God, that mental image does bad things to me," he admits with a laugh. "You in the shower. Hmm." He's staring at Jacob's arm, perhaps thinking of the night before, when he licked along the tanned skin.

At least, Jacob hopes he's thinking about that. He hopes there's no one in the bathroom, either, because he's going to have to relieve the throbbing erection that is biting into his boxers, and he tends to whimper a little too loudly when he comes. He wonders again if he can possibly smuggle Avery into his room, but he doesn't want to chance it. Not if Mike's there. He's got a big mouth and it'll get all over the school by Monday, the fact that they're hooking up, and Jacob doesn't think he can fight everyone.

Another sigh, and Avery pulls away from him. It's a slight gesture but enough to say he better go. "Tonight, then." He turns and heads for his own dorm.

Jacob takes the stairs two at a time to his floor. He still wants a goodbye kiss.

When Jacob gets out of the shower, clean and damp, flushed from the hot water and his own hand, Mike is back.

"You just get in?" he asks, even though Jacob's wearing only a towel wrapped around his narrow waist and his hair is plastered to his scalp. It's obvious he's been in the shower. Mike's wearing his school uniform.

"No." Jacob opens his closet door and stands behind it as he pulls out shorts and a T-shirt to wear. No uniform for him today. Not on a Saturday. He takes the towel from his waist and rubs it over his hair. The cool air prickles his naked skin. He wishes Avery were here and not Mike.

Mike doesn't look at him. Jacob's found that most guys try to ignore other guys, particularly when they're dressing. He won't lie—he looks. He can't help but look. He's interested in what's curled in the front of men's jeans and he's always looking at that. Even if a boy's fully dressed, he looks. He particularly loves sweat pants. They're better than leather in a lot of ways... they show everything. He thinks Avery would look damn sexy in a pair of sweats.

"You have fun at the party?" Mike wants to know. He's only making conversation.

Jacob hasn't forgotten that he's not speaking to him. "It was okay." Like he's not still thinking about it.

"You stayed all night?" Mike asks.

"Jesus." Jacob drops the towel to the floor, then tugs on a pair of boxers and another tank top. He doesn't feel like wearing more. Pushing the closet door shut, he flops on his bed and sighs. "You're too fucking nosy, Mike."

Mike frowns. "You don't have to curse."

Jacob pulls his sheets over his head. "I'm going to sleep." He's not going to listen to this.

Mike falls silent. Jacob knows Mike's watching him, probably even pouting slightly, but he ignores his roommate. He remembers the way it felt to lie in Avery's arms. He doesn't think his bed has ever felt as cold and alone as it does right this minute. It's too early to say anything, but he thinks he's in love.

Part 2

Chapter 1

Avery thinks Jacob is hot. Not the hottest guy he's ever been with, but he's heading that way. A few more years and he'll stop traffic, if he keeps those curls and that smile he's got. And that body. Damn.

He's never had a boyfriend younger than himself. The last guy he was with, Greg, had been his own age, maybe a few months younger, that's it. Greg was tall and lanky and reminded him of a wolf. It was his dark eyes, his slow grin, the way he loped when he ran. He'd been on the school's track team and was Avery's roommate last year at St. Thomas Aquinas. Avery hadn't been surprised when he didn't come back. They broke up before classes ended for the summer.

But Jacob... Avery doesn't know what made the boy look his way but he's glad Jacob did. That first day of classes he sat on the altar, stared out at the congregation, and wondered what he would do this year. Greg was gone. There had been no one over the summer—no one memorable, at any rate. And the rumors that started last year still plagued him.

They know. Or rather, they suspect, the students do, that he likes boys, and they resent him for it. He's old enough to know it isn't something one admits to freely, not if he doesn't want the shit kicked out of him, so he doesn't say anything. Problem is, Greg hadn't been quiet. He had a loud laugh and a quick temper that flared for any reason at all. He was a lot like Jacob in that respect, always fighting. The only time he wasn't loud was during sex.

One more year, Avery had thought while up on the altar. His gaze slid over the blank faces of the students and that's when he saw Jacob, leaning out into the aisle to get a good look at him. At him. So frank, so audacious. That was when Avery knew he would get with that boy. He had to.

And then he did get with him, at Parker Reid's party. This promises to be a good year.

It's not long before they're inseparable. Every morning after mass, Avery walks Jacob to his first class. He wants to hold Jacob's hand or kiss him and he hates the fact that he can't. They have to be careful. After his lunch, Jacob waits for Avery outside, and they talk for a minute before he races off to class. If it's raining, he waits just inside the cafeteria doors, peering out the small window with a slight frown on his face until he sees Avery. Then he smiles, brightening the whole day. Avery loves that smile more than anything else. He hates to see it disappear.

When classes are over at three, he waits for Jacob on

the path between the school building and the dorms. If
they hurry, they can make it back to Jacob's room a full
ten minutes before Mike arrives. Some days they don't get
that much time. A few stolen kisses while Jacob changes
out of his school uniform, that's about it. When Mike
unlocks the door, Jacob's in jeans and already on his way
out. He carries books like he's going to study. He tells
Mike not to wait up for him, he'll be out late. "Where?"
Mike always wants to know.

"The library," Jacob always replies.

But first they stop by Avery's room so he can change,
too. If they're lucky, Avery's roommate Timmy Coleman
won't be there, but he always is. He glares at Jacob from
the safety of his desk because he doesn't like Jacob. He's
told Avery as much. Timmy is one of those who thinks the
school shouldn't let in boys like that, but when Avery asks
what exactly he means, Timmy can't say. He thinks Avery
is a fool to hang out with Jacob. He thinks Jacob doesn't
have long at St. Thomas Aquinas. "I'll be surprised if he's
still here after winter break," Timmy says.

Avery hopes Timmy is wrong. Jacob isn't a bad kid.
He's randy, yes. Stubborn and scrappy too, but Avery
knows most of it's just an act. He's only sixteen. He hasn't
learned yet that he can't change the way people think
about him with just his fists.

Eventually they end up in the library, in one of the
private study rooms students can use. Maybe they even
study some. But mostly it's hungry kisses and eager hands
thrust under shirts, through opened shorts. Avery has
memorized the feel of Jacob by now. He knows the shape
of the bulge that strains Jacob's boxers. He knows the
contours between Jacob's legs. He's caught the fine hairs
on the back of Jacob's wrist countless times in the teeth

of Jacob's zippers. He quite likes the way Jacob whimpers whenever Avery touches him. This is what Avery is studying this year, this boy. He thinks if his finals are on the erogenous places along Jacob's neck, or how to leave him aching with a kiss, then he's going to pass with flying colors.

There's an old tree outside the school building, in the courtyard where Avery waits for Jacob after class. Avery doesn't know what kind of tree it is—the nuns call it a cucumber tree, but he's not sure why. It's a huge, sprawling thing that's been on the school grounds since the church was first built back around the turn of the century. The cucumber tree is rounded and full now, but the leaves are starting to yellow. It's already October, and Avery sits on one of the low branches as he waits for his boyfriend. Boyfriend… he likes the sound of that. It's been a while since he could call someone that.

The branch he sits on is so heavy, so ancient, that it's propped up with wooden blocks. There are a few other branches around the tree like that. They're huge and low to the ground, and would crack away from the trunk if they weren't supported.

He watches the students file past, heading for the dorms to change. After classes no one's in a uniform if they can help it. Every boy who passes has an armful of books because midterms are just around the corner. Avery should study, too, but he's got time. His grades are good anyway. He's not going to study tonight.

Tonight he's going to take their relationship to the next level.

It's been what, five weeks now? Something like that. And they've kissed until their lips were swollen and sore. There hasn't been another night like the one they shared at Parker's party, but Avery wants more. And he knows Jacob does. He feels it when they touch. He hears it in Jacob's breathy moans. But when can they get together? They both have loser roommates who practically live in the dorms, and the study rooms at the library are only so private. They have blinds over the windows but no locks on the doors. So it's been kissing and heavy petting and once or twice he managed to lick through the flap in Jacob's boxers, but that's it. When they're together, there's so much tension in the air between them, he's surprised they don't spontaneously combust or set the whole damn school on fire. The tension clings to him like static. He spends most of his shower every night releasing it.

So tonight he's going to suggest something else. Something other than the library. He's not sure what yet, but he's been thinking all day and he knows he doesn't want to settle for his hand again. Not tonight.

Warm hands cover his eyes. He grins as he hears Jacob say, "Guess who?"

He reaches behind him and touches Jacob's leg. Careful, his mind warns, but he leans back against Jacob anyway. "The Pope."

"The Pope better get his own boy," Jacob says, mock anger in his voice, "and keep his hands off mine."

Jacob uncovers Avery's eyes and sits down beside him on the branch. Avery turns to smile at him. He loves Jacob's intense eyes, so blue, so deep. Jacob's curls need to be tamed and Avery's hands itch to smooth them down. "Missed you," Jacob whispers.

Avery watches the way Jacob's mouth moves around

the words. He's never felt lips as soft as Jacob's. Greg had thin lips, nothing like Jacob's, which are full and pinked and taste like Chapstick. He wants to feel those lips on other parts of his body, not just his own mouth, his face, his hands. That's why they need to be alone tonight. If only the school would disappear.

"Missed you, too," Avery sighs. Jacob's the only thing he's been thinking of today.

With a leer, Jacob asks, "We gonna study tonight?" His hand brushes against Avery's thigh as if by accident. The brief touch burns through his pants to brand his skin.

Avery laughs. "You know it. Come on." He stands, stretching like he's been sitting for too long, but he just does it because he likes to see Jacob's eyes widen as his khakis pull tight across his butt. He knows he has a nice ass. He likes it when Jacob tells him so.

When he starts toward the dorms, Jacob hurries to fall into step beside him. Their hands brush as they walk, they're that close. Avery wants to take that hand in his and hold it tight. He wants to shove it into his pocket and let Jacob feel just what it is the boy does to him.

"I bombed my geometry test." Jacob keeps his voice down and looks only at Avery. He's gotten good at ignoring the other students. There have been no more fights since that first one last month. When nothing else happened, the kids stopped talking about it. Even the nuns aren't watching over him so closely anymore. "How was your day?"

"Better now," Avery says with a wink. "We studied for that test. What did you get?"

"A fifty-two." Jacob grimaces. "I know we studied. Jesus, Avery, we sat up for hours last night."

Avery nods. They did stay up late, the math book open in front of them, but Avery doesn't remember much of the text. He remembers trying to explain sine and cosine at about the same time Jacob's fingers found the zipper of his jeans. After that the rest of the evening is a jumble of kisses and numbers in his mind and it's no wonder Jacob didn't do well on the test. They were too busy studying each other to learn much about graphs. "Maybe you would do better to study alone," he suggests. He's only half serious.

The stricken look on Jacob's face makes him laugh. "I'm teasing." He bumps his elbow against Jacob playfully. "Jacob, I am."

"You better be," Jacob growls. "I ain't studying by myself."

Leaning closer, Avery whispers, "That's what your hand is for."

Jacob grins. "I'd rather it be your hand."

"It will be," Avery promises. "We're gonna get it on, baby, don't worry."

Jacob's grin threatens to split his face, it's so wide. Has Avery mentioned he loves that smile? Because he does. This time as Jacob's hand brushes his, Avery catches the fingertips in his palm and squeezes them quick before he lets go.

"God," Jacob sighs. The word is a rush of hope. "Avery—"

"I like you, Jacob." Avery says it low so no one will overhear him. "A lot. More than I've liked anyone in a long time."

"I like you, too," Jacob whispers. "I'm glad we haven't done much more yet, though."

Avery frowns. He wants to do more. They're together,

aren't they? He believes that in relationships, affection is shown through sex. They've been playing around for a while now, testing each other, but it's leading up to more. He knows it is. He wants it to. And he thought Jacob did, too. "Why not?"

Jacob shrugs. "I've fooled around," he says, trying to sound nonchalant. Instead, he sounds scared, like Avery will run away because he won't like what he has to say. "Just rushed into things, I guess. Never really had a boy of my own. Not like…"

Avery wonders what he's trying to say. Jacob just shrugs again. "Not like you." One corner of his mouth pulls up in a partial grin. "I guess I just didn't want to jump the gun, you know? I didn't want to fuck around and then have you disappear on me like all the other boys I've known."

They're at the dorm now. Avery stops at the foot of the stairs and catches Jacob's hand again. Jacob takes one step, two, then looks back at him, frowning. "I'm not going to disappear," Avery tells him. "If you don't want to get too involved—"

"I do," Jacob says. His voice is so earnest, Avery has to believe him. "God, I do."

Then he clues in on what Avery's not saying, and he gasps. "Oh, wait. You mean tonight?"

Avery nods.

"Thank you, Jesus." Jacob's eyes flash with excitement as he rolls them heavenward. Before Avery can release his hand, Jacob tugs on it to entice him to follow.

With a laugh, Avery lets him lead the way upstairs. He can't wait until they're in Jacob's room, behind the locked door. He's never wanted to kiss someone more in his whole life than he does right now.

Chapter 2

Mike isn't in. Jacob tosses his books on the floor by his bed and strips out of his blazer, then begins to unbutton his shirt. "I hate this damn uniform."

Avery sits on the edge of Jacob's bed, watching him undress. He's not surprised to see Jacob isn't wearing an undershirt—he says he likes the way the fabric rubs against his nipples during the day. "Makes me think of you." It's only been a month since they met, but Avery already thinks he's in love.

Jacob kicks off his shoes. He unzips his pants and drops them to the floor. Avery loves his legs. They're tanned and covered with fuzzy blond hair. When Jacob wears shorts, Avery rubs his hands up and down Jacob's legs, feeling the hairs stand up beneath his touch. Jacob laughs when he rubs the hair the wrong way. He says it tickles.

In his boxers and socks, Jacob leaves his pants on the floor and opens the closet door to get something more comfortable to wear. A sweatshirt and jeans, maybe, since there's a chill in the air now. Before he can dress, though, Avery snags the waistband of his boxers and reels him in close.

"A kiss first," he says, wrapping his arms around Jacob's waist.

Jacob cradles Avery's face in his hands and laughs. It's an infectious sound, bringing a smile to Avery's lips. "A kiss?" Jacob leans down until their foreheads touch. "Is that all you want?"

Avery's hands slide into Jacob's boxers. He cups Jacob's buttocks with both hands, squeezing lightly. Jacob's skin is smooth and cool beneath his palms. Avery has never touched it before. He doesn't think he'll ever stop.

Another squeeze, this one insistent. He pulls Jacob toward him for a kiss and Jacob straddles him, pushing him back to the bed. Avery lies down as Jacob climbs over him. His lips find the shelf of Jacob's collarbone and he bites it with a playful nip that makes Jacob laugh again. "You know what I want," he breathes. They both want it.

"Right here?" Jacob asks. It makes him excited and aroused when they talk about sex—Avery sees it in his eyes. They sparkle like dew. "Mike might come in…"

"Let him." Avery's fingers slip below Jacob's buttocks, where he touches skin as soft and supple as worn leather. "We'll give him an education he won't soon forget."

Jacob giggles. Whenever he gets to thinking about the two of them doing it, he giggles. Avery finds it infuriatingly cute. It turns Avery on.

Between them, Jacob's already turned on, hard and horny just from the mention of sex. He's an eager boy. He rests his head on Avery's shoulder. "I want to," he sighs. "I want you to be my first."

"I will be." Avery already knows that. It's just a matter of time.

He kisses Jacob's neck. Tiny kisses at first, and he licks

along the curve of Jacob's throat as if the skin is spun of sugar. Jacob tastes that sweet.

Avery rolls Jacob back against the wall, trailing kisses across Jacob's smooth, boyish chest. He pulls Jacob closer. His mouth closes over one hard nipple as ruddy as Jacob's lips. He swirls his tongue around the bud. It's like those button candies he used to buy as a kid. Colored nubs on white cardboard. Lick them off. He can do that now, eat this boy up like that. He wants to.

Jacob's sharp intake of breath is a hiss in the quiet room. "Where did you learn that?" Jacob always asks things like that. Avery doesn't like to talk about the guys he's known but Jacob always wants to know.

"My first boyfriend," Avery replies. He bites Jacob a little harder than he intends to. He thinks they should change the subject.

Jacob moans. His hand fists in Avery's hair, tugging just until it hurts, then relaxes. "Greg?"

Avery thinks he asks because he's insecure. He's never had a boyfriend before; he says that over and over again, as if he's amazed Avery would even like him. Avery can't understand that... what's not to like?

But Avery knows the name of every boy Jacob's ever been with. He's gotten play by play commentary on every blowjob. He knows about every kiss. Sometimes he wishes Jacob wouldn't tell him about it all, just surprise him with something Jacob's learned along the way, but Jacob has to tell him. It's like confession. Like Jacob can be washed clean if Avery forgives him.

In Avery's mind, though, there's nothing to forgive.

He shakes his head. "Not Greg."

"Who?" Jacob wants to know. His fingers twist in Avery's hair. "You said Greg was your first."

"He was." Avery doesn't want to talk about this.

Apparently Jacob does. He pulls Avery's hair gently until Avery looks up at him. He's frowning. "You just said…"

Avery sighs. It's a bother to think about this shit. It's the past. He's not with those guys now; he's with Jacob. "Greg was the first guy I slept with. My first boyfriend…" He shrugs. "We just fooled around. Like you and your boys." He doesn't want to say it was the first guy he ever got off other than himself. He doesn't want to say it was the guy who gave him his first blowjob. "Jacob—"

"How old were you?" Jacob asks.

Avery thinks they're wasting time. At any minute Mike will be back and Jacob will have to get up and finish getting dressed. Avery wants to get as far as he can before that happens. He wants more than touches and kisses and he wants more now. "Jacob—"

But Jacob has other ideas. "How old?" he presses.

"Fourteen." Avery shakes his hair free of Jacob's grasp. "Can we keep going here? Please?"

Without waiting for a reply, Avery kisses the hollow of Jacob's throat. He knows Jacob's thinking. He can almost hear the thoughts.

Fourteen. Jacob's thinking Avery was a freshman at St. Thomas Aquinas at fourteen. He's thinking… "Does he still go here?"

You haven't met him, Avery wants to say, but that would be a lie. "You don't really know him," Avery says instead. He knows that's a mistake when Jacob pushes back to frown at him again.

"Was it Parker?" he asks. Of course he'd think that— he remembers the party and that's the only person Avery introduced him to.

Avery laughs. "Parker's straight," he says. "Remember Marie? Parker likes girls. He's into tits, not dicks."

Jacob looks as if he doesn't believe him.

Avery sighs. "Tyrone. At the party?"

"Him?" Jacob laughs. "Damn, he went here?"

"He was twenty at the time," Avery says. "Not a student."

"You fucked around with a twenty year old?" Jacob's incredulous. Avery remembers when he thought twenty was ancient, but it's only three years away now. It doesn't seem so distant anymore.

"I didn't fuck him." Avery doesn't like the way Jacob's staring at him, mouth open. "Jesus, Jacob, I'm almost twenty now."

"Almost," Jacob points out, "but you aren't, not yet. You aren't even legal. Besides, when you're twenty, I'll be nineteen and it won't be so bad." He brushes Avery's hair back from his face. The bangs stand up as if shocked. It's the gel Avery uses that does that. "Twenty. Damn."

"Okay," Avery says. He's had enough. He rolls off the bed, kicking Jacob's books by accident as he stands. "Get dressed. We have to study."

"Avery, no." Grabbing Avery's arm, Jacob pulls Avery into his arms. "Don't be pissy. I'm just playing." He kisses the spot right in front of Avery's ear where the hair is cut short and stubbly. "Don't be mad."

Avery laughs. How can he be mad at this? He struggles to sit up but Jacob holds him down. "I'm not," he says. "I just don't want to talk about it. What's the use? That's so long ago. Years ago. You're my boy now."

"What did you call Tyrone?" Jacob asks. Avery can hear the grin in his voice. "Your old man?"

"Jacob," Avery warns.

"I'm kidding," Jacob tells him. Avery wishes he could show Jacob there's no reason to dwell on the guys he knew. They're out of the picture now. Jacob's the only one painted in.

Avery leans back to kiss Jacob when there's a knock at the door. It's Mike, propping his books against the door to unlock it. The door knob twists as if Mike expects it to be open. He should know better—it's always locked when it's just Avery and Jacob alone. "Jacob?" Mike calls out, his voice muffled through the wood. "I can't reach my key…"

"Fuck." Jacob lets Avery sit up, then climbs off the bed.

Avery scoots back against the wall. The bed sheets are rumpled beneath him. He hopes Mike doesn't notice.

Jacob unlocks the door but doesn't open it. "Get your ass in here," he growls. He's picking up his clothes from the floor when Mike enters the room.

"Thanks," Mike breathes. His hands are full of books. Mid-terms. Avery thinks he should be as studious. When Mike drops the books on his own bed, he turns and notices Avery on Jacob's bed across from him. "Hey." He never says Avery's name.

"Hey." Avery stares at him for a long moment.

Mike shifts uncomfortably beneath his gaze. He glances at Jacob, who's dressing, and then quickly looks away. "I got an eighty-six on the geometry test," he says. Avery knows he's not bragging—he just has nothing else to talk about. Avery thinks Mike doesn't like the silence in the room.

"Woo fucking hoo," Jacob tells Mike. Avery hears the rustle of clothes as Jacob shakes them out but can't see him. He's on the other side of the closet door now.

Mike looks hurt. "What about you?" He glances at Avery again. "What did you get?"

"None of your goddamn business," Jacob says. Avery knows he swears just because Mike hates it.

Avery holds up his hands, one open flat, the other with two fingers raised.

Mike frowns. "Eight?" he asks, counting. "You got an eight?"

"It's seven," Avery says, surprised Mike passed the math test. He opens and closes his hands as if flashing the numbers. First the open hand, five. Then the other one, two.

Jacob peeks around the closet door. "Don't tell him."

"You got a seven?" Mike asks. "Is that possible?"

"It's fifty-two, moron." Jacob slams the closet door shut. He tosses his clothes at Avery. "I told you not to tell him."

Mike's still frowning. "I thought you studied…"

"Shut up." Jacob tugs on a white T-shirt. His back is to Mike and he's looking down at Avery with a wicked smile on his lips. He puckers up and blows Avery a kiss just because Mike can't see. When Mike starts to speak, he warns, "Ah, ah, ah! I said shut up."

"You're mean," Avery whispers. He stretches out his leg and taps Jacob's thigh with his foot. "Be nice to your roommate. He'll slit your throat when you sleep. Then he'll get straight A's for the semester."

It's a rumor the freshmen like to spread. If your roommate dies, they think you automatically pass everything. The stress of coping with the loss, or some such nonsense. As far as Avery knows, it's not true. The only student Avery knows who ever died at St. Thomas Aquinas was a boy with bone cancer, but his parents took him out of school before he passed away and his roommate was transferred to another room. Avery doesn't think that kid got instant A's.

"He's already getting A's," Jacob says. Avery thinks he might resent Mike for that. "He doesn't need to kill me for them."

As Jacob steps into jeans, Mike turns away so he doesn't see Jacob dressing. "You shouldn't bother to change," he says. "We have mass at eight."

"What the fuck?" Jacob turns, confused. "I went to church this morning, thank you very much. I ain't going again." With a wink at Avery, he adds, "I got studying to do."

"Feast of the Most Holy Rosary." Mike looks past him at Avery and shrugs as if he doesn't want to be the one to remind them. "It's required."

Chapter 3

Avery forgot all about the mass. It's not a holy day of obligation for the Catholic church, but it is for St. Thomas Aquinas Boarding School for Boys. All students must attend because they each have a rosary. It's like a compass in other schools, something you have to buy, even if you're not Catholic. Even though Avery is, he's never used his.

The thing tonight isn't even a mass, not really. There's no Eucharist, just a few readings before the monsignor blesses the rosaries. Then he prays on the beads, singing every other prayer in Latin. If they're lucky, the whole thing will be over before 9:30. That'll give Avery and Jacob a half hour before lights out to fool around.

But Avery wants to do so much more than what a half hour will allow.

He wonders if maybe tonight's not a good night after all. He feels bad about Jacob's fifty-two, as if it's his fault his boyfriend bombed the test. It is, partly, and he knows Jacob needs to study tonight for the French oral tomorrow. Avery knows Jacob sucks at French. No, he thinks as they leave Jacob's room, where Mike is already leaning over his desk, studying. Tonight's not a good night at all.

They swing by Avery's room to check the lay minister schedule. Avery hopes he's not serving this evening. If he's the altar boy, he needs to be at the church an hour before mass and there goes more time he should be spending with Jacob. At the next minister's meeting, he has to tell the nun in charge of the schedule that he doesn't want to serve more than once a month, if that.

But he's not on the schedule for the rosary service. Thank God. Since they have mass later, he doesn't bother to change out of his uniform. Jacob's back in his school uniform, too, but the shirt is untucked and unbuttoned at the neck, and Jacob's blazer is draped over one shoulder the way some of the preppier boys wear theirs. Avery likes the look.

They don't go to the library right away. Instead, they sit outside in the courtyard by the church because it's nice out. This is part of their routine. They'll stay here under the shady trees, sitting on their blazers with their books sprawled around them, until the cafeteria opens. Then they'll eat an early dinner. After that they'll head for the library and the privacy of the study rooms. Avery thinks if Jacob had studied geometry on the courtyard instead of waiting until after dinner the night before, he might have passed the test. They do study when they're outside. They have to—too many other students sit out on the grass, too. They can't do anything out there.

But Jacob doesn't feel like studying just yet. He lies back on the grass and watches the clouds through the branches that stretch above them. Avery leans over his psych book, open in his lap. Every now and then Jacob's fingers pick at the place where Avery's shirt is tucked into his pants. Once or twice they slip into the waistband because it puckers at the small of Avery's back. Avery hopes no one is watching them. There's a sycamore behind them, though, so maybe no one can see what Jacob's doing.

Avery keeps his book pressed against his stomach, partly to hide his budding arousal, partly because it feels good to have it pushing against the hard thickness in his pants. "You need to study," Avery tells Jacob. "Vous devez étudier." He finished up with French last year.

"I will," Jacob says.

"En Français." Avery doesn't want to see him flunk out of St. Thomas Aquinas. Then he'll go back home and Avery will never see him again. Avery's determined Jacob will study.

Jacob's quiet for a long time. Avery thinks he's just being ignored. Finally Jacob whispers, "J'étudie bientôt."

"J'étudierai," Avery corrects. "You will study, not you're studying now."

"That's what I said."

Avery looks at Jacob over his shoulder only to find his boyfriend grinning.

"What?" Jacob asks. His fingers slip into Avery's pants again. This time he works Avery's shirt up a little. His touch is warm along Avery's skin. "I'll study soon. Okay? How's that?"

"Why not now?" Avery asks.

Jacob shrugs. "I want to watch you."

Avery laughs. "All I'm doing is studying," he says. "Like you should be."

"Yeah, yeah, yeah." Jacob's fingers ease beneath the top of his briefs. He rubs a soft spot in Avery's skin, just above his tailbone. "Do you like this?" His voice is quiet.

Avery laughs again. "You better stop it," he warns. He doesn't want Jacob to stop, though—he likes the way it feels. But there are other kids around. He's sure someone sees them.

"I can touch my boyfriend, can't I?" Jacob sounds petulant. Avery thinks he might be pouting so he doesn't answer. He doesn't know what to say.

Jacob doesn't press the question. Instead, he sings to himself, so low Avery can't make out the words. Avery wishes Jacob would study. He's going to fail French as well as geometry if he isn't careful.

Some time later, Jacob asks, "How did you meet Tyrone?"

Avery sighs. "That's history," he says. "Old history, not the kind Sister Mary Catherine teaches. You won't get quizzed on it."

"I want to know," Jacob says.

"I don't want to talk about it." Avery doesn't. He hasn't thought about Tyrone in a long time. When he saw Tyrone at the party, he felt nothing for the man he used to date. Nothing at all.

But Jacob's tenacious. "You told me about Greg."

Avery should say he only did that because Jacob asked. Jacob wanted to know if Avery had sex before and when he said yes, Jacob had to know all about it. The boy's name, how they met, why they broke up, where Greg was now. Avery didn't know the answer to that last question. Greg was his roommate last year. Avery didn't remember exactly why they hooked up, just that they did, and one thing led to another. It was easy to be together, too, since they shared a room. Jacob thought they fucked every night, but it wasn't like that. They started dating in November of Avery's junior year and didn't even share a bed until after midterms in March.

Then one of the priests caught Greg and another boy

in the showers at the gym. Avery didn't say another word to him after that. Their room was quiet the rest of the semester, too quiet, as if they had both already moved out. When school let out for the summer, Avery went home and Greg never called. Greg didn't come back this year. Avery thinks that's not such a bad thing.

With Tyrone, it was different. "We met at the mall." Avery's still reading his book, pretending he's not thinking about boys he used to know. "I told you, I never slept with him."

Jacob's hand slides beneath Avery's shirt to trail up the bony nubs of his spine.

"Just sucked each other off, is that it?" He giggles like he does when he thinks about Avery and sex in the same train of thought.

Avery doesn't think it's funny. He thinks Jacob's asking because they haven't done much more than kissing and touching. He thinks this is Jacob's way of hinting they should do more now. Avery couldn't agree more, but he wishes they didn't have to bring up his old boyfriends to talk about it. "You're just saying you want us to get around to doing that too, aren't you?"

Jacob giggles again. It's a cute sound. Avery wants to throw his book aside, lie down and press his boy to the grass, kiss his clothes off, and show Jacob what it is Avery dreams of doing. "Right now?" Jacob asks.

So Avery isn't the only one thinking about it.

"Not right now." Avery laughs. "Wouldn't that be a good picture for the yearbook? You and me getting it on right here on the court in broad daylight."

"I wouldn't mind," Jacob says. Avery turns toward him; they're both grinning now. "When, Avery?"

"Soon." Avery turns back to his book but psychology

no longer interests him. "I was thinking tonight but we have mass."

"Fuck." Jacob's silent as his fingertips trace intricate designs into Avery's back. Then he asks, "Why did you and Tyrone break up?"

Avery sighs. "Jacob—"

"That's the last question," Jacob tells him. "I promise. Last one."

Somehow Avery doubts that. "He left me for someone else."

Jacob laughs. "Someone younger?" When Avery doesn't answer, he stops laughing. "I'm sorry," he says. "I didn't mean—"

"It's okay." Avery shrugs off the memory of the pain he felt at the time. It's an old wound, a dull ache. It doesn't mean anything to him anymore.

Jacob's hand eases around his waist. "I'm not going to leave you for someone else," he says. He's so earnest, Avery thinks he probably believes that. "I'm not going to fuck around on you, Avery. I'm not, I swear it."

Avery presses his lips together. He doesn't say anything. He's old enough to know they might not stay together forever, but there's a childish part of him that wants Jacob to be his. To be only his.

A little before five, Avery closes his book and stretches. The cafeteria opens soon. He wants a quick bite to eat and then the library. He can't wait to get Jacob alone in one of those study rooms. That little rubbing number Jacob's been doing to Avery's back has turned him on something fierce. "Dinner time," he says. He leans back on the grass beside Jacob and resists the urge to touch Jacob's face. "Come on."

A group of freshmen walk by, heading for the cafeteria. They're laughing and suddenly Avery thinks it might be at him. He tells himself he's being stupid but he hears their whispers as they pass. "Faggots," one of them says. The word's soft, barely there. If he doesn't look at them, he can pretend it was never said at all.

But Jacob's face clouds over like the sky before a storm. "Fuckers," he spits. He sits up, glaring at the freshmen. One of the boys looks back over his shoulder at them, grinning. "Come back here!" Jacob calls out. "I'll kick your ass, motherfucker. Say it to my face."

"Jacob." Avery catches his arm before he can stand. "Don't."

"Fucking assholes," Jacob mutters.

"Don't fight," Avery tells him. "Jacob—"

"I hate this," Jacob announces. "So I like boys. So what? I like you. Fuck them all." Before Avery can say anything, he raises his voice after the freshmen. "Fuck you all!"

Avery gathers their books together. "Stop it," he says, angry. "You want to be sent to the monsignor's office again? They'll suspend you for cussing, Jacob, don't think they won't. If you get sent home, what the hell am I supposed to do, huh?"

Jacob pouts, still glaring after the freshmen. "I won't be sent home."

But Avery shakes his head. "You will, Jacob. We can't be together if you're not here."

Jacob looks at the ground and doesn't meet Avery's gaze. Avery touches his arm. "What the hell do they know anyway? You're right, fuck them. They're only freshmen, for Christ's sake. Don't let them get to you."

Jacob sighs. He shoves his hands into his pockets and kicks at the grass. "Fuck them."

"Don't get into fights," Avery tells him.

Jacob nods, but doesn't answer.

Chapter 4

Afore dinner, they find an empty study room on the fourth floor of the library. Avery likes to keep to the upper floors of the building, three through five, because there are fewer students there. Most of the kids who study at the library tend to settle on the second floor. There are rows of study carrels there, about fifty or so. When they're all filled, it gets a little too noisy to study. Even for a library.

On the fourth floor, there are only a handful of carrels. Upperclassmen tend to come here. Avery likes that because upperclassmen tend to really study. The library isn't a social place for them. They don't look around and see who else is there. They don't look up from their books; they don't talk to each other. They aren't paying attention to Avery when he draws the shades in the study room. Upperclassmen are at that stage where they just want to get out of school. Avery was there himself until he met Jacob.

There's a short table in the study room. Four chairs crowd around it, two on one side, two on the other. It's one of the smaller rooms. Avery has learned that they aren't usually disturbed if they stick to the small rooms.

It seems someone's always looking for one of the larger ones to use.

Jacob props up one of the chairs under the door knob. He does that every night, and Avery doesn't have the heart to tell him that only works in movies. The back of the chair is too short to catch on the knob and keep people out. But once he's satisfied it's in place, Jacob grins at Avery. "We're finally alone."

"You have French to study." Avery sits down at the table and opens his English book so he doesn't have to see Jacob's sudden pout.

"Avery!" he cries. "I want a kiss."

Avery laughs. "Come and get one. Then you study."

Jacob leans across the table. "You don't really want to study, do you?" He presses his lips against Avery's mouth.

"You need to," Avery says. "Vous ne passerez pas le Français."

"What the fuck does that mean?" Jacob asks.

"See?" Avery counters. "You have to study." He places a hand on Jacob's chest to push him back. He's so warm against Avery's palm. "Sit down."

Jacob sinks into the chair across from him. "I know all I need to about French," he says, his voice sullen.

"French kissing doesn't count." Avery flips through his English text, looking for Hamlet. "If it did, you'd get straight A's."

Jacob grins. "Thank you. I've had the best study partner for that. My own private tutor."

Avery laughs as Jacob's foot nudges his under the table.

"Can't we fool around just a little bit?" Jacob asks. He still hasn't opened any books yet.

Avery looks at his watch. It's almost six. They have to be at church by eight. "We'll study until 7:15," he says. "Then we'll fool around."

"That's not much time." Jacob sighs. "How about 'til seven?"

Avery thinks about it. "Okay," he concedes. "Seven."

"How about 6:30?" Jacob asks.

Avery frowns at Jacob's innocent smile. "Now you're pushing it. You really need to study."

Jacob sighs again. "So you keep saying." He drags his French book across the table as if it weighs a hundred pounds. "I'm jumping over this table at seven. You know that, right?"

Avery laughs. He can't wait until then himself.

Every ten minutes, Jacob asks, "Is it seven yet?" He flips through his French book. Avery knows he's not studying.

Avery reads another line of Shakespeare before he replies. "Not yet." He's stopped looking at his watch when he answers. He knows it's not time.

Ten minutes later. Jacob asks, "Now?" Exactly ten minutes since he last asked. It's uncanny. Avery wonders if he's counting the seconds off in his head.

"No," Avery tells him. "Not now."

Another ten minutes go by. This time Jacob asks, "Quelle heure est-il?"

Avery is impressed. "Il n'y a pas sept heures." He grins at the look of confusion that crosses Jacob's face. So he takes his watch off and sets it between them on the table. "There. Now you don't have to keep asking."

Jacob frowns at the watch. It's not even 6:30 yet. Avery thinks the boy will never make it to seven.

When ten more minutes are up, he expects Jacob to ask him for the time again, just to be difficult. But he doesn't. Avery waits, sure he's going to say it. He's got a reply all ready. He'll act a little ticked and say something like if Jacob really doesn't give a shit about his grades, then Avery doesn't care, either. Then he'll put his book aside and push his chair back from the table. He doesn't think Jacob will be able to sit on the other side all alone for long after that.

But Jacob doesn't speak. Avery is almost disappointed. Avery glances up from his book only to see Jacob bent over his own like he's finally decided to buckle down and study. Jacob's head is propped up with one hand, his fingers laced through his curls, and he's not looking at Avery or the watch. Just staring at the book.

Good. Avery leans back in his chair, returning to the Bard. He only has a few more pages to read tonight, anyway. He's not sure he likes Hamlet, though. It's too depressing.

Something brushes against Avery's leg beneath the table. He frowns. Jacob's still bent over his book, ignoring him.

Avery feels it again, a foot rising up his inner thigh. Then soft toes press into his crotch. Kneading. Teasing. Stroking. Pushing, just slightly, just enough to get him going. He closes his eyes against the shivers radiating through his body. When he opens them, he expects Jacob to be watching him, smiling.

He's not.

He's still studying, as if he's not aware of what his foot's doing to Avery under the table. Avery thinks this is fun, this pretending, so he's not going to say anything, either. He won't be the first one to crack. Instead, he sinks a little lower in his seat until the foot is flat between his legs. He holds his book up in front of him, so Jacob can't see the way his lips part when those toes dig into the hardening bulge in his pants. When Jacob tries to pull away, Avery squeezes his legs closed a little to keep the foot in place.

Across the table, Jacob snickers. Avery tries to read but it's the same two lines, over and over again. "How weary, stale, flat, and unprofitable," Hamlet tells him, "Seem to me all the uses of this world." Avery thinks his eyes are stuck. He tries to move to the next line but Jacob's toes tickle against his zipper and he goes back to the top of the page like the carriage return on an old typewriter. "How weary, stale, flat, and unprofitable..." Avery is thinking Hamlet needs to get laid. He's thinking if Hamlet had someone like Jacob, Hamlet wouldn't be so quick to kill himself in the end.

When Jacob presses into him again, harder this time, more insistent, Avery slips a hand beneath the table. He closes it over Jacob's toes, which wiggle through his sock. Avery doesn't let go. Jacob breaks the silence first. "It's seven."

"It's not." Avery lowers the book to look at the watch. It's only quarter 'til.

"It is." Jacob pushes his heel into Avery's groin. "I know you want to."

"Want to what?" Avery thinks Jacob's going to say fool around. He's waiting for that. He'll say yes, you're right, I do.

But Jacob grins. "Stop studying." He tries to pull his foot away.

Avery holds it tighter. "No," he teases. "I could study

all night long."

Jacob sighs. "Well, I can't." He pushes the French book away from him. "All the words just run together. I don't know what I'm reading." He looks at the book propped up in front of Avery. "What are you reading?"

"The same two lines," Avery says. "Over and over again."

"Oooh, fun." Jacob twists his foot free from Avery's grasp. Standing, he leans across the table, pulling the English book down. "Kiss me again."

"Is it seven yet?" Avery knows it's not.

Jacob pockets the watch so Avery can't see it. "Yes," he lies. "Kiss me."

Avery laughs. "Hey!" He reaches for the pocket but Jacob catches his hand and pushes Avery's book aside. "That's my watch."

"Come and get it," Jacob says.

Avery likes the challenge he hears in Jacob's voice. When he stands, Jacob backs away a little, eyeing Avery as if trying to guess which way he's going to come around the table. Avery suspects Jacob will run the other way. But he doesn't want to chase his boy. If they're not going to study until seven, then he's got a few ideas of how he wants to spend the next hour before mass. Ideas that involve Jacob in his arms and not trying to get away from him.

So he does what Jacob's not expecting. He kicks off his shoes and raises one knee to the table. Jacob's eyes widen as Avery climbs onto the table. He moves like a lion stalking his prey, crawling across the table, his gaze fixed on Jacob's mouth. Rawr.

On the other side of the table, he brings his legs around over the edge to sit down. Jacob takes another step back but Avery knows his boyfriend won't give chase. It's not on Jacob's mind to run anymore. Avery thinks Jacob's in shock like a rabbit caught in headlights, frozen in his gaze. When Avery eases off the table, Jacob moves back only one more step. The back of his knee hits the chair propped against the door and Jacob falls into it almost gratefully.

Avery leans down over Jacob, a hand on either side of the chair's back, hemming Jacob in. Jacob looks up and swallows with an audible click. Avery leans down further. His nose brushes against Jacob's cheek. "You have my watch," he whispers.

Jacob nods. He doesn't speak. Avery lets one hand trail over Jacob's shoulder, down his chest, across his crotch. Avery grins when his fingers press into hard flesh sheathed in khaki. "Is this it?"

Jacob moans in reply. Of course, it's not the watch. Avery feels around just to make sure and wants him more than ever. "Avery," Jacob manages. His hands fist in Avery's shirt.

Avery kisses his neck. He likes the way Jacob smells this close, the lingering scent of Jacob's sporty cologne. He kneads Jacob with his fingers the same way Jacob did to him, with his foot, beneath the table. His other hand fumbles for the light switch by the door.

He finds it. The room is plunged into a cool darkness. The only sounds are Jacob's sighs, which Avery muffles with his kisses. So much for studying.

Chapter 5

Avery likes to take it slow. He likes to begin with kisses, each one promising more. Then his hands—he likes to touch. He doesn't start below the belt like many other boys seem to do. There are so many places to linger over between the mouth and waist, too many places that demand to be kissed or caressed. Below the belt it's a few minutes of hard pumping and it's over. Avery likes to take his time. He doesn't like it to be over so soon.

In the hour before mass starts, he lets his hands explore Jacob. He could just do it and get it over with already, but where's the fun in that? He likes the tension that stretches between them. He likes the way Jacob gasps each time his fingers open another button on Jacob's shirt. It takes twenty minutes just to get them all undone. By that time Jacob's unzipped his pants only because they've grown too tight across the crotch. Even though Avery wants to, he doesn't let his mouth move lower than Jacob's nipples. They're in the library, he reminds himself. They can't just get it on right here, right now.

Besides, he likes the torture too much.

By the scant light peeking through the blinds, Avery

can see Jacob's flushed cheeks, slick with sweat. His lips are open, slack. When his eyelids flutter, his eyelashes cast long shadows across his face. Each nipple is a dark maroon nub ringed with red, swollen flesh. Avery sucked each one until they grew too tender to touch. Avery suspects they could probably cut glass, they're diamond hard right this moment.

At Jacob's crotch, his boxers bulge obscenely through the open fly of his khakis. When Avery's hand brushes over the underwear accidentally, his fingers come away damp. He knows Jacob will be loud when he comes tonight.

Part of him feels bad. This is his boyfriend he's bringing to the edge of desire and lust, showing him what it's like to glance into the abyss of release, but he doesn't let him jump in. He knows what Jacob's feeling—his own pants chafe him until he wants to scream. They should just give in already. If nothing comes of tonight, they'll both die from blue balls during mass. He's heard it can happen.

But there's another part of him, the wicked part Jacob says he can see in his eyes, that likes this. He likes making Jacob ache for him. He likes wanting him so bad that his dick throbs like it was crushed in a vicious hand. He knows when they finally do get past this point, it will be amazing, for them both. He wants Jacob's first time to be memorable. Avery can't even recall his first, and he sure as hell doesn't want Jacob to ever forget about him.

At quarter to eight, Avery pulls away. "We better get going." He flicks on the light before Jacob can protest.

Jacob's shirt is open, his pants unzipped. He grips the

seat of the chair as if he's in danger of falling off. Avery suspects he's closer to falling than he realizes.

Through his open fly, his white boxers are wet to an almost translucent shade. He's leaning back in the chair, eyes shut. His breathing comes in quick, hurried pants. "Avery," he whispers. "Please."

When Avery stands, he shifts his own erection so it sits more comfortably along his leg. It hurts just touching it. He thinks his pants are going to rub holes right through his balls. "We have to get to mass."

Jacob moans. "I don't want to go," he says. His voice is hoarse. "Can't we—"

"We'll get in trouble," Avery tells Jacob. A skipped holy day service without a physician's slip is simply asking for it. He did it once his freshman year—skipped All Souls' Day for a Halloween party Tyrone had invited him to. That earned him a day's suspension. He doesn't need another one on his transcript when he graduates.

He straightens his shirt, which has pulled free from his pants. He doesn't tuck it back in. "Come on." Avery leans down over Jacob and kisses him once more, tenderly but without their previous passion. He tugs at the zipper of Jacob's khakis.

As the zipper bites into him, Jacob moans again, louder.

Avery pushes down on the thick hardness and tries again. "Come on, Jacob," he says. "Think about your mother." The bulge beneath his hand softens. He laughs as he pulls up the zipper all the way.

"You're evil." Jacob struggles to sit up but doesn't quite make it. Avery can't wait to see him this exhausted and weak after sex. "Make me so damn hard and just walk away. I see how you are."

"I don't want to." Avery kisses his chin as he buttons Jacob's shirt.

Jacob doesn't move to help him. "Then let's go back to my room." When Avery's lips cover his, he moans again. Avery thinks Jacob's getting louder each time he does that. "Mike will be at mass. We can get this over with already. Please?"

It's tempting. So tempting that Avery catches himself thinking one more suspension won't look too bad on his transcript. But he shakes the thought away. "We need to at least show up." If only to scan their student IDs in the vestibule so the nuns know they came to mass. Maybe they can slip away after that. If no one sees them…

"Come on," he says again. He stands and slaps Jacob's thigh to get him moving.

Jacob looks at Avery for a long moment. Then he sits up again. This time, he makes it. He shrugs his shirt so it settles better along his shoulders. A slow grin starts to pull across his lips. "You've got that look in your eyes," he says. "What are you thinking?"

"That we're going to be late." Avery busies himself with gathering their books. He didn't realize Jacob could read him so well.

"It's your I've got an idea look." Jacob stands, pushing in the chairs around the table, then opens the blinds. He looks like he slept in his uniform, it's so wrinkled. "Tell me."

"Not yet." Avery tosses Jacob his blazer. He doesn't want to say anything just in case it doesn't work out. They might be seen in the church. They might not be able to get away.

"You're thinking we can skip the service somehow, aren't you?" Jacob's grinning like the Cheshire Cat. When

Avery turns away, he still sees that grin in his mind. "Tell me, Avery. Please."

Avery scoops his books up in one arm. Tossing his blazer over his shoulder, he opens the door. A rush of cool air washes over him. He hadn't realized they generated so much heat. He sees the window is a little steamed up. They have to be more careful.

"Come on," he says again. He heads for the elevator, Jacob right behind him. He's not sure what his plan is, but it involves getting Jacob alone during mass because it will just be the two of them then. Everyone else will be at the service. Somehow he's got to get him alone.

The ID scanners look like those things stores use to swipe credit cards. They're at every door of the church, a nun nearby watching to make sure they're used correctly. Avery wonders how else you could use it. You stick your student ID in upside down, it slides through, you pick it up when the machine beeps. It's not brain surgery.

He waits for the beep. The nun watching over him is Sister Mary Something or other, Avery isn't sure exactly what her full title is, but she teaches Driver's Ed to the juniors. He didn't have her class. He had Father Sean, who is hell on wheels. That was before they transferred the priest to the biology labs.

When the machine beeps, he smiles at the nun. She doesn't smile back. Maybe she doesn't want to be at the Feast for the Most Holy Rosary, either. Or maybe she's just hot. It's October and finally getting cool out late in the day, but she's dressed in a penguin suit like all the other nuns on the school grounds. Instead of smiling, she tells him, "You boys are late."

Behind him, Jacob runs his ID through the scanner. "Yes, ma'am," Avery says with a nod. "We were studying." Her frown deepens until it threatens to slice into her neck. She's older than his mother and the way she looks at Jacob suggests that she thinks their being late is all Jacob's fault. She's heard Jacob is a troublemaker.

The machine beeps a second time. Avery hurries away from the nun, sure Jacob's right behind him. "Where are we going?" Jacob's voice is a little too loud—it echoes in the vestibule.

Avery doesn't go through the doors to the nave. He can see the pews of boys already seated, waiting for the service to start. Another five minutes, he thinks, no more. If they're going to sneak away, they have to do it now.

Without turning around, he knows Sister Mary Something or other is watching them. "Avery…"

"The bathroom." Avery glances over his shoulder. The nun has turned away, ignoring them now. "Let's go."

Jacob follows him through the heavy doors that lead to the restrooms and the hidden parts of the church the students don't usually see. Avery knows his way around back here because he's an altar boy. He's familiar with these "behind the scenes" hallways. He knows what's on the other side of most of the closed doors. Their shoes echo on the tiled floor. When they pass the bathrooms, Jacob starts. "Avery—"

"Hush up," Avery says. No one else is around but he doesn't raise his voice. He knows where they'll go now and he doesn't want anyone to find them. He catches Jacob's arm, leaning close to whisper in his ear. "Trust me."

Jacob nods. Beyond the restrooms, Avery pushes

through a door that reads Stairs. He knows where this staircase goes. He waits until Jacob closes the door behind him before he starts down the steps.

Without another word, Jacob follows him. Avery likes that. Down one flight of stairs. Through another door, this one unmarked. They're below the restrooms now. Jacob looks around, wide-eyed, because he's never been in this part of the church before. Few students have.

Avery leads him through a double set of doors to the chapel. It's directly below the main nave and it isn't really a chapel—it's not consecrated. It's just where the choir practices on Thursday nights. Avery used to sing in the choir, but since he's met Jacob, he hasn't been to practice. He really should go. He's the only bass at the school and he likes singing. Besides, it pads his transcript, too. But he doesn't have the time anymore. Jacob takes up all of his time now. He wonders what Father Fred, the choir master, would have to say to that.

The chapel has no more than five pews ringing a small altar. Once Avery closes the door, Jacob asks, "Do they use this?"

"Not much," Avery tells him. "Just the choir, for practice."

"What did they use it for?" Jacob sinks into the last pew.

Avery drops his books to the seat and pulls Jacob to his feet. "Private services, mostly. Leave your books here." Jacob sets his books on top of Avery's. "Confessions, too, if you don't want to talk face to face with the priest in the new confessionals. They have the old booths down here."

"They don't." Jacob's face lights up like a kid at a carnival, about to witness something he's only heard of before but has never seen—the bearded lady, maybe, or the world's only living unicorn. "I thought that was just in movies and shit." His hand clamps over his mouth. "Forgive me."

"It's okay," Avery tells him with a wink. "It's not consecrated, so you can cuss if you want." He grins. "Want to see the confessionals?"

The way Jacob laughs, like he's overly eager but scared at the same time, says that's exactly what he wants right now.

Chapter 6

There are three dark wooden doors along the back wall of the chapel. These lead to the confessionals. Well, the two on either side do. The one in the middle is where the priest sits. When Jacob asks if it's just like on TV, Avery tells him yes. "Little screen and all," he says. "So he doesn't see who you are and you can tell him all the horrible things you've done."

"Not me." Jacob shakes his head for emphasis. "I haven't really done anything bad. Nothing worth confessing, anyway."

Avery raises an eyebrow at that. "Oh, no?" He wonders why Jacob's told him all about the boys he's known then. If that's not confessing, he doesn't know what is.

He opens the last door on the right. "Come in," he says with a grin, sweeping his arm at the dark maw that stretches before them.

Jacob grins back. "This is cool." His voice echoes as he steps inside.

Avery enters behind him. It's crowded with the two of them in the booth, and Avery feels Jacob's butt press against his crotch, but they fit. His libido flares to life again at the brief contact. Jacob throws open the tiny window that separates their booth from the priest's. "You talk into here?" he asks in a low whisper. He presses his lips to the screen. "I'd like fries with my salvation, please."

Jacob giggles. Avery smiles at the sound, so breathy, so close. Behind him, he fumbles for the bolt in the dark. When he finds it and slides it home, the scrape of metal on wood is impossibly loud in the tiny room. Jacob turns to him, eyes wide in the scant light that filters through the screen. "What was that?"

"Me," Avery whispers. His hands find Jacob's waist. "Just locking the door."

Jacob giggles a second time. Avery lets his hand cup Jacob's crotch. He's hard again, just like that. He slides the window shut when Avery squeezes gently. His moan comes out between clenched teeth like a whimper.

"You can scream here as loud as you want." Avery presses his lips against Jacob's ear as he speaks. "No one will hear you when you come."

"Avery," Jacob sighs. It sounds like a sob.

Avery works down the zipper of Jacob's khakis. He unsnaps the damp boxers, pushes the flaps out of his way. Jacob's knees buckle, sinking him onto the plush bench that rests against one wall of the confessional. Avery kneels before him. Forgive me, Father, he thinks randomly, for I have sinned.

"We can't," Jacob whispers, but his push against Avery's shoulders is halfhearted at best.

"Why not?" Avery eases Jacob back against the wall. Jacob slides down a little, legs spreading apart. His feet rest on either side of Avery's knees. Leaning on Jacob's thighs, he asks again, "Why not, Jacob?"

Jacob seems to have forgotten how to reply.

With long, slow strokes and gentle kisses, Avery brings

him to where they left off in the library. It doesn't take much time at all, and then Avery takes it a step further, just as he had hoped. When Jacob gasps his name, it's a breathless litany that fills the confessional, like fifty Hail Marys or twenty Our Fathers. "Avery," he sighs, over and over again, "Avery. Oh, Avery. Jesus, Avery." It's the first time Avery has ever been called "Jesus" before.

Jacob's hands grasp at Avery's hair. His moans fill the confessional. Avery wonders if anyone upstairs in the nave can hear them. Jacob is loud, just as he had told Avery he would be.

When they're finished, Avery kisses away the sweat above Jacob's upper lip, his hands smoothing across his boyfriend's flushed brow. He got what he wanted tonight—a taste of his boy. He's going to have Jacob on his lips all night long.

When they leave the chapel, Jacob can't stop grinning. He keeps covering his mouth to stifle his giggles. His hands touch Avery's waist, his back, his wrists. He can't seem to walk straight. "God," he sighs.

Avery laughs.

In the stairwell, Jacob presses Avery against the wall, their books between them where Avery clasps them to his chest. Jacob's hands hem him in, one on either side, keeping him in place. He kisses Avery's throat and growls, a sexy sound that makes Avery laugh again. "Jesus, Avery," Jacob whispers. His lips are hot on Avery's skin. "I mean, holy fucking cow. Damn." He slips his arms around Avery, pulling him closer. He's forgotten someone could find them here.

"No one's ever done that to you before?" Avery can't help but smile. Jacob's cheeks are still pinked. "I thought you said you've had boys—"

"Not like that," Jacob tells him.

Avery wants to ask what made it different, but he thinks he knows. It's the fact that they're in church, for starters, and the fact that they want each other as badly as they do. The past few weeks have been leading up to this. How could it not have been good? "My turn next," Jacob murmurs against Avery's neck. His hands rub along Avery's waist to ease around his back. "I'm going to blow your mind. Make you forget all about Greg and Tyrone and anyone else there was—"

"I've already forgotten them," Avery tells him. When Jacob's mouth closes over his, he breathes, "There's only you, Jacob. Only you." Before he can stop himself, he adds, "I love you."

He falls in love easily. Always has, always will, he supposes. He doesn't like to, but that's just the way he is. He told Tyrone he loved him two weeks after they met. Tyrone laughed. Avery remembers how impish he sounded, like he thought it was a cute thing to say. The day he called and Tyrone told him he wouldn't be picking him up anymore, he vowed to never be the first to say the words again. But he did, to Greg, the first time they had sex. And what was Greg's reply? "I know." Avery hasn't ever heard the words said in return. Sometimes he thinks he never will.

For a minute Jacob stiffens against him and Avery wishes he could take the words back. He wishes they weren't true, but they are. He loves this boy, he knows it. He wants to tell Jacob he doesn't have to say it also. He doesn't expect him to.

But Jacob surprises him. "Really?" He pulls away a little, just enough to look Avery in the eye. There's a slight frown on his face, like he thinks this might be a joke and he's not getting the punch line yet.

"Yeah." Avery hopes this doesn't scare Jacob off. He's only sixteen, his mind whispers, but he ignores it. "I do, Jacob. You don't—"

Jacob laughs. Not Tyrone's condescending laugh. Not Greg's cocky I know laugh. It's refreshing like water, that sound. Avery allows himself to smile at it. "I thought it was just me," Jacob says.

Avery frowns. Now he's the one who doesn't get it. "What do you mean?"

Jacob's hand caresses his cheek, his fingers soft like butterflies along Avery's skin. "I didn't think you liked me that much," he says. "Every night when you walk me back to my dorm? I want to say it. I want to hold your hand and gaze into your eyes and tell you I love you, but I'm scared. I was scared, terrified of what you'd say or do. I thought you'd push me away, maybe. Tell me we were getting too serious too soon."

He watches Avery closely. His thumb strokes a smooth path along Avery's jaw. Avery feels as if every inch of him leans into that touch. Suddenly he can't think, can't breathe, as if he's fallen into a pool and is sinking fast. Drowning in Jacob's gaze. It's the scariest—and the most amazing—feeling in the world.

"God," Jacob sighs. "I love you, Avery. I do. I love you so much it's like someone's stabbed me, right here…" He points to his heart. "Just looking at you hurts sometimes. Does that make sense?"

Avery knows exactly what he's talking about. "Perfect sense."

"Then tell me again," Jacob says. "Please."

Avery grins. "I love you." He laughs. He likes the sound of it. "I love you, Jacob. Okay? I love you."

Jacob giggles like he does whenever they talk about sex. "I love you, too."

Avery thinks he's never heard anything quite so wonderful before.

Chapter 7

In the morning right before his alarm rings, Avery dreams of Jacob. He dreams they're back in the confessional, only this time it's him on the bench with his pants undone. Jacob's hands and lips are driving him crazy. He's so close to coming, so damn close. When Jacob says he loves him, it's almost enough to throw him over the edge. A few seconds more...

His alarm clock shatters the dream.

He rolls onto his stomach, groggy with sleep. The dream clings to him like Saran Wrap. The mattress presses against his aching groin, sending slivers of sweet pain shooting through his lower back and thighs. He hasn't woken up this hard in a long time.

"You gonna turn that thing off?" Timmy calls out.

Avery opens one eye to see his roommate already half dressed and sitting at his desk, bent over a last minute assignment. Without a word, he shuts off the alarm and burrows deeper beneath the covers. He tries to will away his erection, thinking about his sister, his mother, the damn nuns in their black and white habits like extras in an old film. He needs to pee something fierce but he's not getting out of bed until his shorts don't tent out in front of him. If only Timmy would leave for five minutes. Hell, not even that long. Just a few seconds with his hand is all he needs. The dream and the memory of Jacob from the night before have already gotten him started.

Sometime later Timmy says, "You're going to be late."

Avery glances at the clock again. Twenty minutes have gone by since the alarm shrieked him awake. He didn't realize he'd fallen back asleep. Now it's almost eight in the morning. Even without a shower, he doesn't think he'll make morning mass.

Someone knocks on their door. Avery pulls the blankets over his head. "Go away," he moans. Maybe he'll skip mass this morning. He still aches from the dream. He wishes he could sleep with Jacob like he did at Parker's party—he'd love to wake up beside him every morning. Then he wouldn't have to dream about him. He thinks if Jacob were his roommate, they'd miss mass every morning. Class too, more than likely.

Timmy opens the door. It's a guy named Brian, a senior from down the hall. He peers into the room and asks, "Avery here?"

Through the thin sheet, Avery sees Timmy point at him. "Lazy ass still in bed," he grumbles. "You get him up."

"He's got a call." Brian talks as if Avery is still asleep.

Timmy shrugs. "Tell him, not me."

Brian steps into the room. "Hey, Avery—"

Avery sits up. The covers fall to pool at his waist. Stretching, he growls when he yawns. He doesn't want to get out of bed just yet. "I got a call," he says. His voice is an octave lower than usual and thick with sleep. "I heard you already. Who is it?" He hopes it's Jacob, even though he doesn't think he'd call this early. He hopes there's nothing wrong.

Brian turns and walks away. "It's for you," he says over his shoulder. Like that's a real answer.

It's not Jacob, it's Parker, and something is wrong. Avery can hear it in his friend's voice when he asks, "Have you missed morning service at all this week?"

Avery frowns. He's in his boxers and an old T-shirt, and he's cold. The hall advisor hasn't turned on the heat in the dorm yet, and probably won't for a few more weeks. Avery thinks he should start wearing long johns to bed.

He sits at the desk by the phone and watches the other seniors rushing from their rooms to the bathroom and back again, hurrying to get ready. Mass is in half an hour. "Not a morning mass," Avery says. He doesn't mention the Feast of the Most Holy Rosary last night. "Why?"

"Get dressed." Parker's voice sounds strained through the phone. Avery doesn't like it much. "I'm coming to pick you up."

"I have class," Avery reminds him. Skipping mass is one thing. He can't just blow off his classes, too. "Things might be different at State but—"

"Avery."

The word silences him. He's known Parker long enough to hear the fear in his voice. He knows this is serious, whatever it is. Carefully, he asks, "Where are we going?"

Parker sighs. He sounds old, much older than eighteen. He sounds ancient, and scared, and alone. "Marie missed her period."

"Shit." Avery closes his eyes. "You don't think—"

"This is the second month," Parker tells him. He speaks softly, as if he's afraid to talk louder. As if raising his voice any will make what he's thinking—what Avery is thinking—a reality.

Avery coils the phone cord around one finger. He remembers Marie from the party, a pretty girl, older than Parker, with auburn hair that he thinks was probably permed. Much older. She thought they were cute together, he and Jacob. He wonders exactly how old she is. Late twenties, he guesses. "So you're saying she's—"

"I don't know," Parker interrupts before Avery can say the word. Pregnant. "I want to buy a test. She's got to work this morning or she'd get one herself."

Avery wonders how accurate a home pregnancy test is. "Why not take her to the doctor?"

"No insurance." Parker laughs, a shaky sound that frightens Avery. "Shit, you think I haven't already thought of that? Fuck."

"Why do you want me to come along?" Avery asks. He's never bought a pregnancy test in his life. Hell, he doesn't even know where they sell those things. K-Mart? He doubts they'd be very reliable on a Blue Light Special.

Parker sighs. "Moral support? Come on, man. I don't know who else to call. I can't go by myself." When Avery doesn't answer immediately, he pleads. "Please?"

"Fine." Avery sighs. "Get over here. I have to be back by 9:30. I have a test in first period."

"I'm on my way," Parker says. Another laugh, this one

almost relieved. "Thanks."

"Just hurry it up," Avery tells him.

When he hangs up the phone, he thinks he should call Jacob and tell him he won't be at mass. But he's late enough as it is, and he still needs to get dressed. He has to pass Goodman Hall on his way to the gate anyway—he'll just stop in and tell his boyfriend where he's going. It'll be nice to kiss him first thing, too, if Mike's not in the room. And if Parker gets him back before mass is over, he can still walk Jacob to his first class. French, with Sister Thérèse, and that oral exam he's going to fail miserably.

Avery hurries back to his room to dress.

He hears the whispers when he steps onto Jacob's floor. Someone laughs. A boy in the hall stops and stares. The kid is wearing boxers, no shirt, but he wraps a towel around his chest when Avery glances his way, like he's got anything Avery wants to see.

On his way to Jacob's room, another boy pushes past him. "Get off me," the kid mutters. His elbow catches Avery in the ribs.

Avery ignores him. He's good at that. He's found that bullies tend to lose interest if he doesn't fight back. That's part of Jacob's problem, he thinks. Jacob can't tune others out. If someone says something to him, he has to talk back. If they shove him, he pushes back harder. Avery wonders if the boys snickering behind him say anything to Jacob. He hasn't gotten in a fight since the first week of classes and Avery thinks his notoriety is beginning to wear thin.

"Fucking queer!"

Avery almost jumps at the shout, which comes from the bathroom, echoing off the tiles and out into the hall. He feels the words weigh him down, feels the stares, hears the laughter. For a second he falters. His foot, in mid-step, forgets where the floor is. These are sophomores, he tells himself. He's a goddamn senior…

Don't.

Hasn't he told Jacob that? Don't.

So he doesn't. He puts one foot in front of the other. He keeps his head high, as if he didn't hear it. As if he doesn't care. Because he doesn't. These boys know nothing about him, or Jacob, or how they are together. If they even knew, they wouldn't be so quick to degrade them or mock the way they feel for each other. Avery suspects half these kids will never feel even an inkling of what he feels when he's with Jacob and for that, he pities them. They'll never know how it is to lose themselves in someone else. Because of that, he's better than they are. Because he doesn't let them get to him. Because he doesn't care. He only cares about two things right now—Jacob and graduating.

He hates to admit it, but some days Jacob's the only thing.

When he knocks on Jacob's door, there's more laughter. Because he doesn't turn around, it sounds louder than before, more daring, more bold. He doesn't care. He tells himself that as he knocks again. I don't care. "Come in," someone calls from inside. Avery opens the door.

Jacob's still getting dressed. He has his khakis on and his shirt half buttoned. He's slicking back his hair, which is still wet from the shower. Avery knows the curls will kink up as they dry, but right now they're dark like brown sugar.

When he sees Avery, he smiles. "Hey!"

Avery knows he's happy to see him. He wishes they were alone. He'd like a kiss to start the day.

But Mike's there, making his bed. He turns to frown at Avery. "Hey."

"Jacob…" Avery starts.

He was going to tell him he's skipping mass, but he doesn't have to say a word. When Jacob looks at his jeans and T-shirt, Avery can almost read the thoughts in his eyes. No school uniform… "Mike." Jacob's forehead creases as he tries to imagine why Avery isn't dressed for class. "Get out."

Mike glares at Avery. "It's my room, too."

"Just for a few minutes, okay?" Jacob glances at him, already pouting. "Go take a piss or something. Please?"

"Jacob," Avery says, "it's okay—"

Too late. Mike brushes by him on his way out the door. When he slams it behind him, Avery says, "You didn't have to…"

He doesn't get to finish the sentence. Jacob closes the gap between them with one step and suddenly his lips crush Avery's in a savage kiss. "I dreamed about you," Jacob sighs. His hands smooth across Avery's chest, fingers pinching hard nipples until Avery gasps his name. "I woke up aching for you. Did I tell you I love you? Did I say that last night?"

Avery laughs. "I believe you did."

He hugs Jacob tightly. He wants to warn him about the boys in the hall but here in the safety of the room, in Jacob's arms, it seems silly to mention it. But he wants to ask if anyone's been bothering him lately. If only he could protect Jacob from the hot whispers and harsh words. If only he could make him understand nothing matters but the two of them, together, and the rest of the world be damned. "I love you, too."

"Then why are you ditching mass without me?" Jacob wants to know. He's grinning faintly, like he's waiting to be asked to come along, wherever it is Avery is going. He probably thinks that's why Avery is here.

Avery sighs. He rests his forehead against Jacob's— he likes the comforting press of their flesh. Jacob's skin is cool and still a little damp from the shower. "Parker wants me to run to the store with him. I'll be back before mass is over."

"Why?" Jacob asks.

"Because I have class, silly," Avery tells him. He knows that's not what Jacob's asking.

"No," Jacob corrects, "I mean why—"

Avery sighs. "He thinks his girlfriend's pregnant." He keeps his voice low, but it still sounds worse once the words are spoken.

Jacob's eyes go wide. "Marie?" As if there might be another one he knows about.

Avery nods. "He wants to buy a pregnancy test but doesn't want to go alone, you know?" Even though Parker didn't ask, he can't help but add, "Do you want to come?"

He thinks Jacob's going to say yes. Parker might not like that but Avery will make up something if he has to. He really wants Jacob to go.

But Jacob studies Avery's face, his eyes flickering uncertainly. Finally he shakes his head. "No." He kisses Avery once more. "You go. You'll be back in time to walk with me to French class?"

"Mais oui," Avery says. He winks at Jacob. "Je t'aime."

Jacob grins crookedly. "What's that mean?"

"I love you."

Jacob's eyes light up, and Avery is sure that's the only French he'll ever remember. He thinks it's probably all Jacob needs to know.

Chapter 8

B uy me something," Jacob says before he leaves.

Avery laughs. "We're going to a drug store, I think."

Jacob shrugs. "I know. Buy me bubble gum." His eyes sparkle at the thought. "Please? God, I haven't had gum in so long." They don't sell gum in the cafeteria, and neither of them has been off the school grounds since the night of Parker's party.

"Bubble gum," Avery says, amused. If that's what it takes to make Jacob happy, then he'll buy all the gum he can find.

Parker's car idles outside the gate. As Avery sinks into the passenger seat, church bells peal into the still morning air. Mass has started. He hopes they can be quick about this. "I have an exam in an hour," he says instead of hello.

Parker revs the engine. It drowns out the bells. "I have a test tonight." He laughs. "A pregnancy test. Shit."

Avery doesn't like the way Parker doesn't look at him.

"Do you really think she's—"

"No," Parker says, a little too quickly. "She doesn't think so, but we've got to be sure, you know? Fuck, we use condoms." He grimaces. "I mean, mostly."

Mostly. Avery knows Parker well enough to know that means they aren't religious about rubbers. The two of them have been friends for going on four years, ever since Avery's freshman year at St. Thomas Aquinas, when they both signed up for the crew team. They were assigned to the same shell that first day, Avery as coxswain, Parker in the bow. He was dangerous with an oar, though, and after almost tumbling into the water, Avery suggested they switch places. "Maybe you can call better than you can stroke," Avery had said.

Parker ended up quitting before the season was through, and Avery didn't try out again the next year, but they stayed friends. Parker was the only person Avery ever told straight out that he was into guys. He even had a small crush on Parker at first, until he realized Parker wasn't that way.

It's hard to tell with Parker, though. He's the type who flirts with anyone, not to hit on them but because that's just the way he is. He's full of fun and has a contagious laugh, charming everyone he meets. The nuns at the school loved him. He could do no wrong.

Avery doesn't remember Parker ever not having a girlfriend. Someone back home who called him every night. Someone who wrote him long letters on pretty stationary. Someone who probably had his name written all across her notebooks. It was Parker Avery went to when Tyrone told him they were through. "He's an ass," Parker had said. "You don't break up over the phone."

Avery felt better because Parker had to know what he

was talking about. Even at sixteen, he already knew more about relationships than Avery does now, three years later. When Greg wanted to have sex, Avery went to Parker for advice. "It's only sex," he said then. "It's fun and feels good. It's not like you're getting hitched, you know? If you want to fuck him, go for it."

That's Parker's philosophy. Only now that's gotten him into trouble, hasn't it? Or Marie, at least. In the side-view mirror, Avery watches the school shrink into the distance and wonders what the hell they'll do if the pregnancy test is positive. Parker's only a year older than he is. He can't imagine being a dad now. He's having enough trouble keeping his mind on school.

Behind the wheel, Parker sighs. "So we forgot once or twice, okay?" He shrugs like Avery is questioning him, which he isn't. He hasn't said a word. "I always pull out. Always." When he laughs, it's a bitter sound that makes Avery uncomfortable. "Damn."

Avery doesn't know what to say. "Maybe you're right," he offers. "Maybe it's just what, a false alarm? Can that happen?" Even with an older sister, he knows nothing about girls.

Parker mumbles, "I think so."

He stares at the road as he heads into town. The stretch is a two-lane highway and this early in the day, they're the only ones on it. Parker doesn't have the radio on. The only sound between them is the steady thump of the tires over tarmac. "Maybe it's something else," he says hopefully. "You know?"

Parker glances over at Avery, who nods not because he does know but because Parker expects him to be encouraging. That's why Parker asked him along. "Maybe it's something else completely."

Avery can't imagine what that something else might be.

The first store they come to is a Rite Aid. Avery has never stopped here before. He thinks after today, he's never going to step foot into this store again.

Parker pulls into the first empty spot in front of the store. It's marked handicap but there's no one around to complain. The only other two cars in the whole lot are both parked at the far end, so Avery thinks they're employees. There's not a cop in sight.

Inside the store is cold, like a meat locker. It's bright, too bright. Behind the counter, two employees, both women, lean against the register, talking. They look up as the door opens, then turn back to their conversation, dismissing them.

"So," Parker starts. He looks uncomfortable in the bright lights. He frowns at the aisles that stretch away from them. "Where do you think they keep these things?"

Avery doesn't know. "Why don't you ask?" He grins at the look Parker throws his way.

"Very funny." Parker doesn't smile. Instead, he heads for the first aisle. "Come on."

Avery trails behind him, up and down every aisle. Greeting cards and shampoo and deodorant. Toothpaste and tampons and aspirin. Finally Parker stops. "Here we go."

He keeps his voice low, as if he's afraid the employees at the front of the store might overhear them. He stands too close to the shelf, shoulders hunched. Avery thinks he looks like he's shoplifting.

Avery glances at the shelf. He expects to see one, maybe two different tests, maybe a generic brand that's a few dollars cheaper. But instead, the whole damn shelf is overflowing with boxes, each one marked 100% Accurate or Results in Just Minutes. He wonders how these things work. They look like sticks and he doesn't want to think about where they go. Pluses and minuses and circles and dots... he's confused. "Which one should I get?" Parker asks.

"Hell if I know," Avery replies. "How about the cheapest one?" That's what he would go for. "I mean, if they're all the same..."

"Cheap?" Parker squats down to look at a lower shelf. "You get what you pay for, right? I'd rather get thirty dollar results than ten bucks."

Avery shrugs. "Parker, I don't know." He points to a teal box. "I like this color."

Parker turns to stare at him. The look on his face tells Avery he's not really helping all that much. "It's blue." He speaks slowly, like he's talking to an idiot. "I want one that works, Avery. I'm not buying it for looks."

"Maybe you'll have a boy," Avery suggests, "if you buy a blue one."

"Maybe you can find something else to do," Parker tells him, "while I pick out one of these damn things."

Avery sighs. "Don't even know why you brought me along," he mutters beneath his breath. "You aren't bothering to listen to me."

But he knows Parker didn't want his opinion as much as he just didn't want to do this alone. He knows if the tables were turned, he'd want someone with him, too. But he doesn't like girls, and as far as he knows, he's not going to get any boys pregnant any time soon.

He wanders to the end of the aisle while he waits for Parker to pick out one of the tests. He thinks Marie should really be here, not him. She's a girl. She should know all about these kinds of things. But she's probably scared. Hell, Avery is scared, and it's not even his girlfriend. He's scared for Parker. Parker is too young to be a father. What will Parker do about school?

Avery doesn't want to ask. He's sure Parker doesn't want to think about it right now.

Past the pregnancy tests are pegs of condom boxes. Avery stops and stares at the rows of black boxes. He should buy some condoms, if he's going to get it on with Jacob. Greg had condoms when they did it last year.

Don't really need them, Avery thinks. He picks up a box that reads Extra Sensitive. He wonders what the hell that means. Condoms are birth control, aren't they? It says right on the bottom of the box that they don't prevent sexually transmitted diseases. Besides, he and Greg only had sex what, three times? If that. And Jacob's never done it. Do they really need condoms? At ten dollars a box, he doesn't think so.

But when he puts back the first box, he sees another marked Heavily Lubricated. Without thinking, he picks it up. If there was one thing Greg skimped on, Avery thinks, it was the lube. There are ten condoms in the box, which Avery finds funny for some reason. Ten for ten dollars. That's a dollar a fuck. What a deal.

Parker comes up behind him. "I'm getting this one." He holds out a pink box, EPT written across it. "I've seen the commercials on TV." In an announcer's voice, he intones, "These are real life couples, not actors." He laughs humorlessly.

Then he sees the condoms in Avery's hand and grins.

It's the first real smile he's had all morning. "You and your boy are already like that?" he asks. "How old is he again?"

"Old enough," Avery says. He's going to buy the condoms now, if only because Parker's picking on him. "How old were you when you first had sex?"

Parker shrugs but doesn't answer. Younger than Avery had been, perhaps. "So you're buying the condoms, I'm getting the pregnancy test. God, this is like a bad joke."

At the counter Avery picks up a pack of gum for Jacob. The cashier reminds Avery of his grandmother. He doesn't look at her as she rings up the condoms. "Are you old enough for these?" She has the raspy voice of a lifelong smoker. Avery's cheeks burn with embarrassment.

When she rings up Parker's test, she laughs. "You should've bought those condoms the first time." The other employee, a girl about Marie's age, laughs. Avery wishes they'd both just shut up and let them leave already. With an audacious wink his way, the cashier adds, "You're the smart one, honey. You won't be buying one of these, will you?" She holds up the pregnancy test and grins.

"You're a riot," Parker mutters.

"No ma'am, I won't," Avery says. When he says ma'am, he sounds cultured and Southern. With a wink of his own, he tells her, "I don't think I can get my boyfriend pregnant. Even without the condoms."

Parker laughs. On the way back to the car, he laughs again. "Your boyfriend," he says. "Jesus."

Part 3

Chapter 1

Jacob lies on Avery's bed, hands behind his head, and stares at the stucco ceiling. Avery sits at the foot of the bed, his long legs bent up to his chest. He's leaning back against the side of his closet. Jacob's bio book is open in his lap.

Avery's roommate sits at his desk, studying. Otherwise Jacob thinks he wouldn't have to go over his biology again. If Timmy wasn't here, Jacob thinks maybe he and Avery could be studying each other and not cellular mitosis. He wishes they were in his room. At least then he could kick Mike out.

But Avery doesn't kick Timmy out. Instead, he sits by Jacob's legs and reads out words he expects Jacob to know: zygote and gametes and mitochondria. And all Jacob can think about is the way Avery's foot rests against his knee. They're both wearing shorts, and the press of flesh is maddening.

Avery nudges him. Jacob lets his gaze drift to his

boyfriend. He likes calling Avery that. My boyfriend. He almost let that slip the last time he was on the phone with his mom. She asked about his grades and he told her he had a study partner. When she asked whom, he almost said, "My boyfriend." But he caught himself in time. "A senior," he said. "That guy Avery I told you about?"

"The altar boy?" his mom asked.

Jacob laughed. "Yeah. The altar boy."

"Jacob."

Avery says his name patiently, like Avery knows it's hard for him to concentrate. Jacob notices the place between his legs where his shorts stretch tight against the cushion of his crotch and thinks again how nice it would be if Timmy would leave the two of them alone. He is so ready for sex. Avery keeps telling him they'll do it, they will, they have all the time in the world. But it's November now, and in another month they'll go home for winter break. He doesn't even want to think about next year. He doesn't like the college brochures that are starting to appear around Avery's room as if by magic.

"Jacob?"

He looks up to see Avery smiling at him. It's a wicked smile that suggests he's thinking the same thing Jacob's thinking. That they need to be alone. When he speaks again, Jacob's sure he'll ask Timmy to leave.

Instead, he prompts, "Chromatid."

Jacob frowns. "What?"

Avery sighs. "You're not paying attention."

"I am!" Jacob cries. Timmy snickers from the safety of his desk. Jacob glares at his back. If looks could kill, he thinks they'd already be alone. "Avery," he sighs. He doesn't want to study anymore. He rubs his toes against Avery's hip. "Haven't we been at this long enough?"

"You're going to fail." Avery means the quiz Jacob has tomorrow on this chapter.

Jacob hates biology. He tries pouting. It doesn't work.

Avery turns back to the book in his lap and asks, "How about nucleolus?"

"How about we take a break?" Jacob wants to know. Timmy laughs a second time. Jacob wishes they were alone again.

Avery stares at him with unreadable eyes. "Please?" Jacob mouths the word so Timmy won't hear him. When Avery doesn't respond, he tries, "I love you."

That brings a smile to Avery's face. He blows Jacob a quick, silent kiss. "We'll finish this chapter," he says. "Then we'll take a break."

Jacob wants a break now. "Avery—"

"Will you shut up already?" Timmy glances at Jacob over his shoulder, brow furrowed like a freshly plowed field. "Some of us really are trying to study."

"Fuck you," Jacob mumbles, but he says it low enough that Timmy can pretend he doesn't hear.

Avery nudges his leg again. "Stop it," he admonishes. "He's leaving in a half hour anyway."

Jacob didn't know that. "For what?" His whole body tingles at the thought of Timmy leaving.

"Hall meeting," Timmy tells him. He frowns at Avery. "You should go."

"I'm busy," Avery says with a wink Jacob's way.

When Timmy leaves, Jacob rolls on his side. He props his head up with one hand and gives Avery his most simmering stare. "Avery," he calls, keeping his voice low. He digs into Avery's hip with his feet.

"Is the door closed?" Avery doesn't turn around to check.

Jacob nods. He doesn't think it's locked, though, and Timmy left his keys on his desk. "How long do we have?"

Avery shrugs as he sets the bio book on the floor. "Fifteen minutes, maybe."

He stretches out on the bed beside Jacob. Rolling onto his back, Avery smiles up at him. Jacob loves the way the overhead light shimmers in Avery's eyes. They're an impossibly light shade of green, those eyes, like apple-flavored Jolly Rancher candy. He touches Avery's chest, smoothing out the T-shirt beneath his palm. His hand moves lower, unbuttoning Avery's shorts. The zipper glides down with a sigh.

"Jacob—"

Jacob cuts his name off with a kiss. He loves the way Avery's lips feel beneath his, so soft, so warm. He doesn't want to talk anymore.

Avery's arm slips under his waist and curls around his back to caress the spot right between Jacob's shoulder blades that he can't reach himself. Avery's short fingernails rasp against his cottony shirt. Jacob leans over, pressing Avery down into the pillow with his kiss.

He eases his hand between the cool teeth of Avery's zipper. Beneath his palm, Avery is already stiffening. Jacob likes that all it takes is one kiss, a soft touch, and Avery's ready to go. Cupping the front of Avery's briefs, he squeezes gently, just until Avery moans into his mouth. Avery arches beneath him, pushing into Jacob's hand. Jacob licks along Avery's chin. He loves the sweet taste of

Avery's skin. "How can you sit there reading off biology terms," Jacob asks, his voice quiet, "when you've got this in your pants?"

Avery laughs as he pulls Jacob onto him.

Jacob straddles Avery's hips, folds his hands on Avery's chest, and rests his chin on his knuckles. Between them, their groins crush together with a velvet ache. "I can take care of it for you," he tells Avery. He likes the way Avery feels in his mouth. That night in the confessional was the first time, but definitely not the last. Even though Avery doesn't like to get freaky in the library, Jacob manages to convince Avery a quick blowjob is in order at least once a week. He thinks Avery tastes better than any boy he's ever known.

"Timmy is just down the hall." When Avery talks, his deep voice rumbles through Jacob.

"So?" Jacob thinks that makes it more exciting. They could even leave the door unlocked. "I can be quick. You know that." He doesn't say please. He doesn't want to beg.

Avery grins. "You're bad." He kisses Jacob's nose, his hands on Jacob's butt as he hugs Jacob tight. "You're going to get us in trouble."

Jacob laughs. "Me?" Any trouble they get in together will be worth it.

"Yes," Avery whispers, "you." He kisses Jacob again. This time Jacob sits up a little, just enough to get the kiss on his lips. "You're going to flunk out of school."

"I'm going to have fun doing it," Jacob replies. Avery's hands slip down Jacob's thighs to hoist him closer. His zipper bites into Jacob's crotch. Jacob's dick aches between them. Another kiss, and Jacob says, "I'm not going to flunk out."

"You better not." Avery pushes at him gently. "Get up."

Jacob rolls off him. When Avery sits up, Jacob hooks a forefinger through one of the belt loops on his shorts. "Where are you going?"

Avery doesn't answer. He opens the drawer on his bedside table and rummages around inside for a minute. Finally he pulls something out, shuts the drawer, and lies back down. Jacob cuddles close to him. Their hips touch.

Avery eases an arm beneath Jacob's head. He holds out his hand, closed into a tight fist. "I want to give you something." He's watching Jacob intently.

"What is it?" Jacob takes Avery's hand in both of his and tries to pry open the fingers, but Avery clenches his hand tighter. "Let me see."

"You have to promise me something first," Avery tells him.

He waits. Jacob looks up at him and nods. "Anything." Jacob's nervous all over again, as if this is their first time together. He didn't have to get Jacob anything. Jacob wants to know what it is. "I don't have anything for you—"

"That's okay." Avery kisses Jacob's forehead. Jacob leans back and manages to plant a quick kiss on the underside of Avery's chin before he pulls away. "Promise me you won't wear it here."

"Here?" Jacob doesn't understand. "Wear what?"

"I don't want you wearing it at school." Avery sighs. "Someone might say something."

"What is it?" Jacob wants to know. This time when he pries open Avery's fingers, they unfold like the petals of a flower. In the middle of his palm sits a ring.

Avery's class ring.

It's bulky, like boys' class rings usually are. The stone is a deep green, so dark it's almost black. The facets shine like Avery's eyes. Gingerly, Jacob takes the ring. He's never been given something like this before. He loves jewelry but the school dress code forbids it during the week. On weekends he pulls out his gold chain, his stud earrings, the bracelet that hangs loose from his wrist.

Avery has said he likes Jacob in gold.

Avery's ring is gold. Or rather, golden, that antiqued look that's popular on high school rings. Jacob turns the ring around in his fingers. It's lighter than it looks. On one side is the school crest in miniature. On the other, the Bible and a cross. Every boy at St. Thomas Aquinas gets the same ring. The only thing that they can pick out themselves is the stone.

"You really want me to have this?" Jacob asks, incredulous. He tries the ring on his fingers, one by one. It slips easily onto the middle finger of his left hand. When he holds his hand out to look at it, his vision blurs. He doesn't want to cry but he's never been given a ring before, not by anyone. "Avery—"

Avery kisses him quiet. "Don't wear it here. I don't want you getting hurt."

"I can handle myself." Jacob's voice cracks, but he's not arguing. He's not going to wear the ring except when they're alone or he's in his room. He thinks he'll even sleep with it on.

Chapter 2

A very's ring fits snug on Jacob's finger. He loves it. During the day he keeps it in his closet on the top shelf. When they come in his room after classes are over, it's the first thing he sees when he opens his closet to change. He slips it on and wears it the rest of the night. He doesn't take it off until he's getting ready for his shower in the morning.

Mike doesn't notice the ring. Or, if he does, he doesn't say anything to Jacob about it. Jacob doesn't make a big deal out of it, either. He's heard the mutters in the hall when he leaves his room. He's not stupid. He knows the other guys on his floor don't use the urinals when he's in the bathroom. Like he wants to look at them anyway. They don't even shower in the stall near his.

Once when he went in to brush his teeth, he found the word homo scrawled across the mirror above the sink. It was written in red lipstick, held to the glass with so much force that the lines still had bits of the cosmetic in it like tiny chunks of meat. He doesn't know who wrote it. When he came back to the room, Mike asked him what was wrong. "Shut the fuck up," Jacob growled.

He hates the kids at this school, he really does. For all

their Bible thumping and church going, they're just the same assholes he knew back in public school.

So he doesn't wear the ring where the boys can see it. It's just something between him and Avery, and those other boys would never understand. Jacob's parents wouldn't, either. He knows that already. When they caught him kissing a boy two years ago behind the garage, they were livid. His father took a belt to his ass, as if he could whip the sinful lust from his body. His mother just cried. He doesn't know what's so wrong with liking other boys. Hell, they would shit if they knew how he feels for Avery. He's already decided he won't wear the ring when he goes home for winter break, either.

It's a ritual now. Every morning, he turns off the alarm clock and looks at the ring. He likes the way the stone glistens in the early light, and how it looks on his hand against the white sheets. When he gets out of bed, the first thing he does is take off the ring. He sets it on the shelf in the closet, the stone facing out like an eye watching him. He gets his towel and shampoo, closes the closet door, and goes to take his shower.

After class, he comes back to the room with Avery and puts the ring on. Mike usually takes his time getting back to the room when school's over with for the day. At first Jacob thought it was because Mike's a nerd, hanging out with his friends at their lockers, sucking up to the nuns for extra credit. But now he thinks Mike stays to give him some time alone with Avery. He's sure Mike knows they're together. He knows Mike hears what the other boys say. He's seen the way Mike doesn't look at him when he's not fully dressed, or when he's lying in bed, or when Avery is in the room. And Mike takes his clothes into the bathroom to change.

Sometimes he wishes Mike would just ask him. "What's up with you and Avery?" It wouldn't be difficult. But Mike probably thinks Jacob will tell him it's none of his business, which it isn't, so he doesn't say anything at all. Jacob wonders if the other boys tease Mike about being his roommate. They haven't started talking shit to his face, not yet, but he knows it won't be long. That fight at the first of the year was enough to keep them off his case for a while. He knows there will be another one after winter break, if not sooner. He feels it in the air, building like electrical current before a storm.

He doesn't want to fight. He wants to bring his grades up and have sex with Avery. And not necessarily in that order.

Because it's grown cold outside, they stay in Avery's room before dinner now. Jacob would like it better if Timmy wasn't there but he is, so it's just the same as before, when they sat on the court to study. But at least here they can sit together on the bed. Timmy doesn't say anything about that. Jacob thinks maybe Avery has told him they're together, though Avery swears he hasn't said a word.

Timmy always sits at his desk, his back to Avery's side of the room. He's already hunched over his homework when they come in. Jacob doesn't think he's ever heard him say hello. He just ignores them, or he'll start talking as soon as Avery opens the door, as if they had been there the whole time and he's picking up a prior conversation where it left off. Sometimes when he does that, just starts up when they walk in, Avery says, "What the hell are you talking about, Timmy?" He always winks at Jacob when he says it. Jacob always snickers at that wink.

"You know." Timmy frowns at Jacob because he's laughing. Then he turns back to his book and pretends they aren't even there.

Jacob likes to lie on Avery's bed. He loves to bury his face into the sheets or the pillows and breathe deep. He can smell the shampoo Avery uses. He imagines the two of them between the sheets, curled together, naked. That image does horrible things to him—makes his stomach flutter and his heart race and his hands tremble just slightly. It makes him laugh. When he's lying on the bed and laughing, Avery grins at him as if he knows what Jacob's thinking. As if he's thinking the same thing. Jacob thinks he is.

With Avery beside Jacob on the bed, their legs rest alongside each other. A few times Avery eases an arm between Jacob and the wall and hugs him like that. With their knees up, Timmy isn't be able to see it if he looked. And once, just once, Avery raised his heavy English book in front of them like a shield and kissed Jacob, even though Timmy was still in the room. It was a quick peck, the briefest touch of lips, but it gave Jacob an instant hard-on. His balls ached the rest of the night because they kissed in front of someone, even if Timmy wasn't paying attention. They kissed and didn't care who saw it.

Jacob's lying on his stomach on Avery's bed. Timmy is at his desk, like he always is, and today's Avery is at his desk, studying. Jacob thinks Avery needs to be sitting by him on the bed. He's horny today and really wants to feel his boyfriend's legs draped over his, or Avery's feet smooth along his thighs, or Avery's hands on his waist. Jacob wants to touch Avery so badly right now. His dick hurts where it's crushed into the mattress. He's already had to adjust it once, to get it to lie flat. He can't help it if he's hard as steel right now. He can't wait until after dinner when they get to the library. He knows they aren't going to do much studying then.

But he's got to finish this book for class tomorrow, so he has to read it now. It's a good thing Timmy is here today. He's failing the class miserably, he knows that. Even with Avery helping him, he's going to bomb French.

And this book—he hates it. It's a children's book, so he thinks it should be easy, but it's not. It's in French. Who the hell would write a kid's book in French? Kids can't read English, let alone French. Shit, he's sixteen, a far cry from a child, and he can't read French. The only thing he knows about this story is what he remembers from the cartoon that used to come on Nickelodeon when he was little. Why they ever translated the story into French is beyond him.

He's been on the same page for the past ten minutes. He doesn't understand a word of the text. He looks at the pictures and hopes he can figure out what's going on. But on this page, there's a drawing of a tiny planet with three big trees that cover it completely. Beneath the drawing are the words, "Enfants! Faites attention aux baobabs!" He doesn't know what the fuck that means.

So instead of reading, he stares at Avery's ring. He turns it around his finger. With each spin, he whispers under his breath, "He loves me. He loves me not. He loves me." He's going to keep doing this until someone asks him something. He hopes he's on he loves me when that happens.

He is. "Fuck," Avery says.

Jacob looks up at him, frowning.

Avery sighs. He sees Jacob looking and smiles. It's a disarming smile that lights up his eyes, so Jacob knows it's real. Jacob is the only person Avery smiles for like that. Most times, in class or in mass, his smile is just the shape his mouth makes and his eyes are a million miles away. Once Jacob asked where it is he goes when his eyes cloud over. "Alone somewhere with you," Avery replied. "You're all I think about." Jacob's never heard anything so sweet.

"What's wrong?" Jacob asks him now. Almost unconsciously, he turns the ring the other way, once, as if to lock it into place. Isn't that what kids do with class rings? For luck. Lock it on the last turn. Jacob's locking it for love.

Avery points at the table beside the bed, near Jacob's feet. "Can you get me another pencil?" He holds up the one he's been using for his trig homework. The point has snapped off completely. "Please?"

Grinning, Jacob sits up on the bed. Anything to get out of Le Petit Prince. He leans over, snagging the drawer knob with one hand, and pulls it open. Inside everything rattles to the front of the drawer. Jacob looks in for a pencil.

A black box of condoms sits on top of everything else in the drawer.

A slow smile spreads across Jacob's face. He picks up the box and wiggles his eyebrows at Avery. "What's this?"

He knows damn well what it is. He's hard just thinking about what it is. Condoms. Heavily lubricated. Ten in a pack. Condoms.

Avery blushes a little. "Put it back," he hisses. He glances over at Timmy to make sure his roommate hasn't seen the box.

He hasn't.

Pushing away from his desk, Avery stands and comes over to the table. "Jacob." His voice is low. Jacob looks up at him, an innocent expression on his face. "Put it back."

Jacob grins.

"Jacob," Avery says again. He takes the box from Jacob's hands.

"Are those for us?" Jacob asks.

"I don't know." Avery sticks the box back into the drawer. Jacob's still watching him—a rosy blush colors his cheeks. "Yes."

As he bends to shut the drawer, Avery leans over to kiss Jacob. It's a Smurf kiss, a quick peck, but it's on the lips and Timmy is in the room. Jacob thinks he could come just sitting here.

Chapter 3

He can't get the condoms out of his mind. Later that evening in the library, he asks, "So when did you buy those things?"

Avery shrugs. They're alone in one of the study rooms with the shades drawn. Jacob wants to take care of the throb in his pants but Avery is still working on trig. Jacob hasn't even opened his book yet. He thinks talking about the condoms will get Avery's mind back where it belongs... on him.

"Last month sometime." Avery isn't looking at him. He's busy with fractions. Jacob doesn't like math. Hell, right now he doesn't like anything that isn't the two of them getting it on.

"When last month?" Jacob knows he's pestering. He likes the way Avery's forehead wrinkles when he frowns.

Avery sighs. Jacob smiles at the sound, so lost, so defeated. Avery knows he won't get much math done tonight, not if Jacob has his way. And Jacob almost always has his way. Avery tells him, "When Parker and I went to the store that morning? Before class?"

Jacob remembers. "For the pregnancy test?" Avery nods. "How did that work out?"

"False alarm." Avery bends over his notebook like he doesn't want Jacob to see what he's writing. Jacob peeks over his arm anyway. It's just fractions, though in the margin of the page Avery has drawn a spray of tiny hearts. He sees Jacob looking and points to the hearts. "Those are for you."

"I love them." Jacob takes Avery's hand and kisses the fleshy pad between his knuckles. "I love you. False alarm?"

Finally Avery looks up at him. There's that smile that's just for him. "Yeah. She got her period that day at work. False alarm."

"So she's not pregnant?" Jacob laughs. "That's good, right?"

"I guess." Avery turns back to his math. "I don't know. They broke up."

Jacob watches Avery's pencil move above his arm. His fingers curl around Jacob's where they're still holding hands. "Because he thought she was pregnant? That's mean."

"Jacob," Avery says, exasperated, "I don't know, okay? I wasn't dating her."

"Thank God."

Avery laughs at that. He squeezes Jacob's hand with a tender gesture, then turns his attention to his homework.

When Jacob is sure Avery's concentrating on his math again, he asks, "So you bought the condoms then?"

"When?" Avery frowns slightly and glances at Jacob, as if he's already dismissed the conversation. Then he realizes Jacob's not finished yet. "Oh, yeah. I got them that day."

Jacob imagines Avery above him, naked, erect. He's seen pictures of how to put on condoms. He snickers at the thought of Avery easing into one. He likes that image. "For me?"

"Of course for you, silly." Avery grins crookedly. Beneath the table he nudges Jacob's foot with his. "Who else do you think I bought them for? Timmy?"

"Stop it." Jacob doesn't want to think about Avery with Timmy. Avery is his boy. Even though he knows all about Greg and Tyrone, that was because he asked. He knows Avery doesn't think about them anymore. And he doesn't want to think about Avery with anyone other than himself.

"I'm just teasing," Avery tells him. When he tries to pull his hand free, Jacob holds it tighter. "Let me finish my math, okay?"

Jacob grins. "What if I say no?"

"Then I'll fail." Avery is grinning, too. "And I'll be stuck back in St. Thomas A-Queer-Ass one more year. Is that what you want?"

Jacob's grin widens. He doesn't answer, but he thinks that wouldn't be such a bad thing after all, if they were together here at the school for another year.

A little while later, Jacob asks, "Are you almost done?" He can see Avery still scribbling so he knows the answer already. He still hasn't opened his French book. Le Petit Prince has nothing on Avery tonight.

Avery laughs. "Not yet." He doesn't look up from his notebook.

Jacob suspects he might not be done tonight at all, or at least not before curfew. He doesn't want to go back to his dorm without a little loving. He thinks of that quick kiss when Timmy wasn't looking. His whole body flushes at that.

He waits another fifteen minutes. He can see Avery's watch from where he sits across the table and watches the hands move until they both point around the eight. Quarter 'til. They have to be in their rooms by nine because it's a school night. That doesn't leave much time.

Avery sets down his pencil to reach for his calculator. Jacob picks at the pencil until it starts to roll toward him. He intends to catch it, roll it back, over and over again until Avery takes it away from him. But he's not really paying much attention—he's too busy watching Avery's forehead crease when he frowns at the calculator, like it's wrong and he can't figure out why—and so the pencil rolls between his hands, off the edge of the table, into his lap, and onto the floor. He hears it hit the carpet.

Now Avery frowns at him. "Jacob." He glances up at him without raising his head.

"Sorry." Jacob didn't mean to drop the pencil. He didn't.

Pushing back his chair, he slides off the edge and onto his knees. The carpet is thin and hard. He ducks his head beneath the table. It's dark under here, draped in shadow. Jacob sees the pencil—it's between Avery's shoes. When he reaches for it, Avery asks, "Find it?"

"Yeah." Jacob crawls forward a little, grabs the pencil, and sticks it up between Avery's chest and the table. "Here you go."

Avery laughs and takes it from him. "Thank you. Now get back up here. I'm almost done."

"Good." Jacob lets his hand fall to the small triangle of the chair's seat that peeks out between Avery's legs. Almost absently, his fingers brush along Avery's zipper.

Beneath his hand, Avery stiffens. "What's this?" he asks, playful.

Avery laughs again. "You'll get it soon enough," he promises. "Just two more problems, Jacob. That's it."

Jacob thinks two more problems can wait until later. He's been waiting long enough. Through the heavy denim of Avery's jeans, he massages the cushiony bulge at his crotch until it's hard and coiled like a snake ready to strike. "Jacob," Avery warns. The name is almost a sigh.

Jacob's not listening. His fingers seem to have a mind of their own. They flick open the button, then work the zipper down.

Avery moans Jacob's name, lower this time. He slides a little farther down into the chair. His knees spread apart beneath the table. Jacob rubs against the front of Avery's briefs and Avery's knees clench together, catching Jacob's head between them.

Jacob eases them apart again, his fingers dancing along the outlined hardness at his boyfriend's crotch.

"Jacob."

It's whispered, like a prayer. Jacob sees Avery's hands above him, gripping the table tight. "God, Jacob," Avery sighs. "Jesus."

With his hands on Avery's thighs, Jacob pushes his boyfriend back a little. The chair moves easily on its wheels across the carpet. "Love you," he says, wrapping his arms around Avery's waist.

Avery pulls Jacob up from the floor and into his lap. Straddling the chair, Jacob sits on Avery's legs and gives into his kisses, leaning back against the table as Avery leans into Jacob.

He fists his hands in Avery's shirt, pulling him closer. Their lips meet in a sweet crush that stirs through him with a thrilling rush. He's never told anyone he loved them before. Well, his mom, but that's a given. He's never told a boy before but he wants Avery to know it. He can't stop telling him.

"I love you, too," Avery murmurs. Jacob loves to hear those words. They turn him on more than the talk of condoms or the kiss behind Timmy's back. If Avery only knew what those words did to him, he suspects Avery would say them nonstop.

Chapter 4

Though it's only a little after nine when Jacob gets back to his room, he thinks Mike is already asleep. The lights are out, all except for the small lamp clipped above Jacob's bed. That one shines at the spot where his bed meets the wall. It brightens the wall, the bed sheets, and casts deep shadows around the rest of the room. Mike lies on his bed, rolled onto his side, facing Jacob's bed, and he doesn't move when Jacob comes in. Jacob closes the door behind him as quietly as he can.

He strips down to his boxers and T-shirt. Behind him Mike sighs, a sad sound in the darkness. Jacob wonders what he's dreaming about that has him so upset. He thinks Mike needs to find some friends to hang out with. Mike spends too much time studying or in this room. Mike needs someone to love him, Jacob thinks, shoving his clothes into a pile by his closet. Like I have Avery. He needs someone like that.

It occurs to him he's never heard Mike talk about a girlfriend or someone special back home. Honestly though, Jacob rarely listens when Mike talks about his family because there are just so many people in it, his mom and dad and brothers and sisters... Jacob's lost count because he doesn't have anything like that waiting for him back home. He knows he gets pissed off that Mike has so many people who love him when Jacob sometimes feels like he has no one. No one but Avery.

Sure his parents love him; he knows this. His little brother Johnny loves him, too, in that idolizing way that five year olds have. But they don't love him for who he is—they don't know him. It's the automatic, you're my son kind of love he thinks is tainted by who they want him to be. Brilliant, so they get upset at his grades. Friendly, so they hate his fighting. Straight, so he can't even tell them about his boy. About Avery. How can his family love him if they don't know about the only thing he loves more than life itself?

He wonders if there's a test tomorrow he's forgotten about, if that's why Mike went to bed so early. As he pulls back the sheets on his bed, he glances behind him. Maybe he should've read that book after all.

Mike's staring back at him, eyes glassy and open in the darkness.

"I thought you were asleep." Jacob talks low because the lights are off. His voice is barely above a whisper.

"I'm not." Mike sounds sick, like his head's all stuffed up and he can't breathe right.

Jacob frowns. Sitting on the edge of his bed, he studies Mike for a minute before he asks, "Are you all right?" He thinks of the way the guys have started to tease him within earshot. He wonders if Mike's getting any of that too, for being Jacob's roommate. "Did someone say something to you? Those bastards…"

Mike shakes his head. "My mom called," he says, sniffling. "My papaw died."

"Your dad?" Jacob asks.

"My grandpa." Mike sighs, heartbroken. It's a painful sound. "This evening. Cancer."

Jacob doesn't know what to say. "I'm sorry?"

Mike starts to cry. Jacob's hands twist uselessly in his lap. He doesn't know what to do. "Mike," he says. He hopes he sounds sincere. He's never known anyone who died before. "I'm sorry. I wish…" He lets his voice trail off.

He wishes Mike would stop crying. It's a horrid sound, blubbering like a little kid. His chest hitches with each breath. Jacob wishes Mike had a friend at this school, someone he could call. He doesn't know what to do.

When Mike covers his face with his hands, Jacob hurries to the bathroom. The maids leave spare rolls of toilet paper beneath the sink. They're huge industrial sized rolls, white paper that's more cardboard than tissue, thick and coarse. He grabs one of the rolls. It slips easily around his wrist. The hall is silent as he returns to his room. No one else is up. It's hard to believe that behind his door Mike is crying out so much pain.

"Here." Jacob sits on Mike's bed and tears off a long strip of toilet paper. Balling it into his fist, he hands it to Mike. Cry into this, he wants to say, but doesn't. That would be mean.

Mike sighs as he takes the offered tissue, then wipes his eyes and blows his nose. "Thanks."

Jacob sets the roll down beside him when Mike reaches for more paper. He watches Mike carefully. "Should I get someone?"

He doesn't know whom. The hall advisor? One of the nuns? Hell, if it'll stop the tears, Jacob will track down the monsignor himself, but he doesn't think Darth Vader would be any comfort to Mike right now.

But Mike shakes his head. "My mom called the school." His voice is soft and thin, much more papery than the toilet paper that crinkles in his hands. "She's coming to get me tomorrow morning."

Friday.

"When are you coming back?" Jacob asks.

Mike shrugs. It's a halfhearted gesture. "Monday?" he asks. As if Jacob knows. "I'm not sure. I don't know when the funeral will be." That starts him crying again.

"Do you want…" Jacob sighs; he's so bad at this. "I don't know. Do you want me to hold you, maybe? Will that make it better?"

"No," Mike whispers. "I'm fine."

"You don't sound fine," Jacob points out.

When Mike laughs, it's a jagged, broken sound. "I'm not," he admits. In a small voice, he adds, "Avery might not like it, though."

Avery. It's the first time Mike's said anything that would suggest he knows about them. "I'm not going to hold you like that," Jacob says. "Just give you a shoulder to cry on. Avery would understand."

"It's okay." Mike sighs. "They talk about you, you know."

Jacob glares at the floor. He doesn't have to ask whom Mike is talking about—he means the kids at the school. "I know."

"Just so you do." Mike blows his nose again, loud.

They're quiet for a few minutes. Jacob waits until Mike's tears taper off. When his breathing eases a bit, Jacob asks, "Do they pick on you about it?"

Mike shakes his head. "Not really." Jacob wonders what the hell that's supposed to mean. "It's not like we're… you know, friends or anything."

"I know." Jacob wonders again if he should call someone. "So you think your teachers know? About your grandpa, I mean. Not…" He laughs at the thought. "Not about me and Avery."

Mike rubs the toilet paper across his nose with a harsh rasp. Jacob wishes they had Kleenex or Puffs, something softer. "My mom called," he says again. "I'm sure they'll be told."

"Is there anything you want me to turn in for you tomorrow?" Jacob feels horrible. He can't imagine someone in his family dying, even if they're not as close as he thinks they should be. He visits his grandparents for a week every summer. They live out in the country, on a stretch of farmland that's no longer tilled. He doesn't want to think about his grandpa dying. The man is larger than life itself.

Mike shakes his head. "I'm caught up."

Jacob wishes he could say the same. Because Mike doesn't cry when he's talking, Jacob tries to think of something else to say. "Cancer?" he asks. When Mike nods, he adds, "Do you want to maybe talk about it a bit? Would that make it better?"

With a shaky sigh, Mike whispers, "He's been sick a while. Lung cancer. But I never really thought…"

He sighs again. Jacob's heart twists in his chest. He thinks if Mike would just sit up, he could at least give him a quick hug. Avery would understand. His grandfather died, for Christ's sake. But Jacob's happy Mike thought of Avery's reaction. He's glad Mike knows about them, or at least suspects. He's glad he doesn't have to tell him now.

"I never thought he'd ever die," Mike says. "I mean…"

"I know what you mean." Jacob tries to picture how he'd feel if his mom called and said her father was gone. Gone. Jacob feels tears prick his eyes at the thought so he blinks them away. He thinks back to this past June, when he last saw his grandparents. He remembers his grandpa showing him the new mare he bought, already with foal. He remembers Pop's strong hands, tanned, lined, ancient. He can't imagine those hands stiff and cold and gray. He doesn't want to imagine it. So he won't.

And he's tired of talking about it now, too. "What time is your mom coming to get you?"

"In the morning," Mike whispers. "Before class."

"Before mass?" Jacob asks.

When Mike sighs, Jacob reaches out to touch his leg beneath the thin bed sheet. He thinks Mike will pull away but he doesn't. He lets his hand drift to Mike's knee. It's bony in his palm, not fleshy and thick like Avery's. He likes the way Avery feels, solid and real. Mike feels brittle, frail, as if he's hollowed out of glass and could break if Jacob raises his voice too loud. He squeezes Mike's knee, hoping it's a comforting gesture. He wants to tell Mike it's supposed to make him feel better. He wants to make sure Mike knows Jacob's not hitting on him because he's not and he doesn't want Mike to think he is, but the words are too awkward to say.

"During mass." Mike sniffles and tears off another strip of toilet paper to blow his nose again. "Will you wait with me? Just until she comes?"

Jacob nods. "Sure." If it were his grandpa, he'd want someone to stay with him. But he'd want Avery, not Mike. He wants Avery now.

He doesn't say that, though. He doesn't mention that if Mike is gone this weekend, maybe Avery can stay with him here, in this room. He wants to sleep in his boyfriend's arms again. Right now, he wants to be held. Mike's talk of death has frightened him because he doesn't want to think about it.

So he doesn't say anything at all. Mike falls silent, and Jacob stays on the edge of his bed until he's sure his roommate has fallen asleep. Then he creeps across the room to his bed. He crawls beneath the covers and clicks off the light. In the faint moonlight that peeks between their curtains, he can see Avery's ring on his finger. The stone shines darkly. Jacob stares at it and tries to think of nothing that will make him sad. Nothing at all.

Chapter 5

Mike sits on his bed, a bag packed and resting at his feet. He stares at the floor. Jacob can see how puffy his eyes are now that it's morning. When he woke up a little after seven, Mike was crying again. Jacob's tired of apologizing. He hopes Mrs. Nelson comes to get him soon.

Lying on his own bed, Jacob's already dressed for class. He even wears his blazer, because they have the window open slightly. It's too warm with the heater on, but now that the window's cracked, it's too cold. He wants to leave already. He doesn't like being in this room with Mike, who can't seem to stop crying. Jacob never thought he'd want to go to church or to class but right now? He wants to be anywhere but here.

The knock on the door doesn't come soon enough. Jacob sits up, relieved. It's not quite nine yet. Mike sniffles but doesn't move, as if he hadn't heard. "Come in," Jacob calls. It's obvious Mike's not going to say anything.

But it's not Mrs. Nelson who opens the door, it's Avery. "God," Jacob sighs. He's relieved to see him. "Avery…"

The way Avery frowns at him dries up whatever else Jacob wanted to say. Avery looks at Mike, who's struggling not to cry again. To Jacob, he asks, "Why aren't you at mass?"

Jacob doesn't understand the sudden anger he hears in Avery's voice. "Why aren't you?" he replies. He hates being confronted. It makes him feel inferior. That's why he always fights back.

Another glance at Mike, and Jacob can almost hear Avery's mind working. They're the only two boys left in this building. Mike's dressed in jeans and a T-shirt. It's so obvious he's leaving. Avery can't be thinking they…

"Avery," Jacob says. When he stands, Avery crosses his arms, waiting. "You can't think—"

"Tell me what to think then." Avery's voice is low, even.

Jacob sighs. He wants to tell Mike to leave though he can't, not this time. But Mike's lived with him long enough now that he senses Jacob wants him to go. He stands up, wiping his eyes with the back of his hand. "I'll be right back," he mutters. On his way out, he doesn't look at Avery.

With the door shut, Jacob says, "I'm not Greg." Avery doesn't speak. "I'm not fucking around on you, Avery."

"What's going on here, then?" Avery wants to know. "You're not in church, you don't call or stop by to tell me why not. I manage to slip away and come over here, worried to death about you, and you're just sitting here. With him."

Jacob rubs his forehead. He tells himself Avery is just being cautious. He's been fucked over before and has somehow jumped to the conclusion that Jacob's fooling around on him. But Jacob thought there was more trust between them. He thought Avery knew he was different. He bites back the dull anger that chokes his throat and says softly, "His grandfather died last night." He suspects he wouldn't feel so shitty if he had gotten more sleep.

"Jesus," Avery whispers.

Jacob wraps an arm around his waist, hugging himself because he doesn't like saying the word died. It reminds him of the thoughts he had of his own grandpa, and he doesn't like those thoughts one bit.

Suddenly Avery is there, enveloping him in his arms, hugging him tight. "Jacob," he sighs. "I'm sorry, I didn't know. I'm so sorry."

Jacob rests his head on Avery's shoulder and nods against his neck. He likes the strength of Avery's arms around him. He hugs Avery close and doesn't want to let go.

With a shuddery breath, Jacob tells him, "His mom is coming to pick him up. He didn't want to be alone. I told him I'd wait with him." He presses his lips against Avery's cheek. "You aren't mad, are you?"

"No," Avery says, a little too quick because he had been mad and now he knows there was no reason to be so he's pretending he never was in the first place. "No, Jacob. Not at all. I was just…" He sighs. "I was wrong. I'm sorry. I should've known you're not like that. I know you aren't."

Jacob pulls away slightly. Avery still holds him close, but Jacob eases his arms between them to pick at the buttons on Avery's shirt. He watches his fingers fumble over the white fabric and doesn't dare raise his gaze to meet his boyfriend's. "I was thinking? Maybe, if you want…"

"What?" Avery kisses Jacob's forehead, his temple, his cheek. He wants to make up for his earlier suspicion. "Thinking what?"

Jacob shrugs. "If you want to stay over here? Maybe? While he's gone…"

Now he looks into Avery's eyes, trying to read the expression he sees there.

"He shouldn't be back before Monday," he whispers. Avery stares at him, silent. "So if you want, maybe you can stay here? With me?" He doesn't want to say please but if Avery doesn't say something soon, he will. He'll beg if he has to.

Avery grins. That wicked light shines deep in his eyes. "Can I bring my condoms?"

Jacob laughs. "If you don't, I'll send you back to get them."

When he kisses Avery, he tries to put everything he feels into the velvety crush of lips. Avery moans into his mouth. Jacob eases a knee between his legs, pressing against the hardness already there. He hopes Mrs. Nelson hurries the hell up.

After classes are over, they go to Avery's room first. Jacob thinks there's no use hurrying, they have all night together, but he's nervous and giddy and can't stop thinking about what that unassuming box of condoms means.

He's not surprised to find Timmy already in the room. Jacob lies down on Avery's bed and stares at the ceiling so he won't have to say anything to him. He thinks if he talks, his words will tumble out in a meaningless rush and Timmy will know they're going to do it tonight. Tonight! He can't wait.

"Jacob's roommate is gone for the weekend," Avery

says. Jacob watches him fold a change of clothes into his book bag. "His grandfather died."

"I'm sorry to hear that," Timmy says, sounding anything but. He glances over his shoulder. "Where are you going?"

"To stay the night." Avery doesn't look at Timmy.

When Timmy glares at him, Jacob tries not to smile back. Mine, he wants to say. My boy. Sorry, Timmy. Even though Avery has said Timmy likes girls. He has one back home, or so he claims. Alyssa? Allison? Something like that. Jacob doesn't remember, exactly. He notices there are no pictures of her on Timmy's desk, though. He wonders if she really exists.

"Is that such a good idea?" Timmy asks.

His eyes say what he doesn't. Jacob remembers what Mike told him last night. "They talk about you, you know." He wants to tell Timmy to mind his own fucking business.

Avery simply shrugs. "I think it's an excellent idea." He scoops his toothbrush, toothpaste, and deodorant into his bag. Quickly he slips out of his blazer and sets it on the back of his chair. He kicks off the loafers they have to wear and unbuckles his belt. Finally Timmy turns away.

Jacob grins as Avery changes clothes. He loves Avery's legs, so strong, so long. He loves his round buttocks, the way his boxers pull taut across his ass when he bends to remove his pants. He loves Avery's thick arms, his muscled chest, his stomach. He wants to touch Avery right now, Timmy be damned. He loves the way Avery looks right this second, dressed in a white undershirt and pulling his jeans up over his ass. Tonight can't come soon enough.

Avery steps into his sneakers, then runs a hand through

his hair to straighten it. The bangs stand up, as if at attention. Jacob loves that. Some days Avery's hair seems to have a mind of its own. "Come on, Jacob." Avery grabs his pillow from beneath Jacob's head as he sits up. "Carry this."

"Okay." Jacob hugs the pillow to his chest. With wide eyes, he watches Avery pull open the drawer to his bedside table. He rummages through the contents for a moment, then pulls out the box of condoms. Jacob feels a grin tug at his lips until his face threatens to break. He wonders if ten will be enough.

Avery shoves the box into his book bag. Zipping it up, he glances around the room one more time to make sure he has everything. He stares at Timmy's back for a long moment before he asks, "Do you mind?"

Timmy shrugs but doesn't look at them. "Why should I?"

He sounds mad. Jacob wonders if maybe it's because he can't have his girl here for the weekend. He has to ask Avery what her name is again. Alice? That doesn't sound right.

Then Timmy mutters, "You're just asking for it."

Anger clouds Avery's face. "For what?" he demands.

Timmy shrugs again.

Avery turns away from him. "You know, fuck that."

Jacob bites his lower lip as he stares at Avery's livid features. The fierce pride in Avery's crystalline eyes scares him. He's never heard Avery so pissed. "I don't give a fuck what others think," Avery says bitterly. "I'm not going to let them decide who I love or what I do or who the hell they think I should be."

He pulls Jacob to his feet, propelling him toward the door. To Timmy's back, he says, "I'm not asking your permission, Timmy. I'm telling you. I'm spending the next few nights in Jacob's room. You don't like it? Fine. Tell the nuns to transfer you to another room. Tell them you don't like having a faggot for a roommate. Tell them—"

"I didn't say me," Timmy says.

He's angry, too, and he pushes back from the desk to whirl around and glare at them.

Jacob thinks all this ire must be directed at him. This is somehow all his fault.

"I didn't say…" Timmy shakes his head. "Jesus, Avery! You know I don't care that you're, you know, like that. I haven't said shit about the two of you. I haven't said one fucking word, so don't you get evil with me." He's still glaring at Jacob.

Avery clenches his jaw but doesn't reply.

Into the tense silence, Jacob whispers, "I'm sorry." He's not sure what he's done but he knows it's his fault. This sort of stuff always is.

"Don't be," Avery tells him. When he speaks, it's softly, like he doesn't want Timmy to hear. He nudges Jacob toward the door, his touch gentle. "Come on. Let's get going."

Jacob clutches the pillow tight as he leads the way into the hall. Alecia. That's the name of Timmy's girl back home. Alecia. He wonders what she looks like to be dating a boy like Timmy. He wonders if she knows about Avery and if it bothers her that they're roommates. He wonders if she knows about him, if Timmy has ever said anything about him always coming over. He suspects she'll hear about it tonight if Timmy calls her.

Chapter 6

I'm sorry," Jacob says again. He can't stop saying it.
They're in his room now, their room for the weekend,
and it's Friday night so they don't have to study.
Jacob lies on his back on his bed. Avery is stretched out
beside him, propped up on one elbow. His fingers stroke
through Jacob's curls with an absent, soothing gesture.
They've been lying like this for a while now. Jacob keeps
glancing up at the tiny square packet sitting on the edge
of his bedside table—one of the condoms from the box.
He can still feel the squishy plastic on his fingertips where
he touched it.

Avery tugs at Jacob's curls, playful. "Sorry for
what?"

Like he doesn't know. Jacob sighs. "For making
Timmy mad," he says, though that's not quite it. He's
afraid Avery will start thinking about how much trouble
it is for them to be together. He's afraid the rumors and
gossip will begin to get to Avery. He's afraid Avery will
stop loving him because of it. "For… I don't know. For
everything, I guess."

Avery rests his head beside Jacob's on the pillow. His
hand fists in Jacob's curls, tugging just a little. He presses

his lips against Jacob's temple and laughs, breathy and deep. "It's not your fault," he whispers.

With a shrug, Jacob says, "I know." He's unconvinced.

Avery laughs again. Another kiss, tender. Another soft tug on his curls. "Don't be sorry, then."

Avery's other hand toys with the front of Jacob's shirt. He picks at the hard nipples hidden beneath the material. It's ticklish but Jacob only squirms closer against him.

Catching Avery's hand in both of his, Jacob brings it to his lips and rests it against his mouth. When he nips at Avery's knuckles, he makes Avery grin.

Then he looks at the condom again. He can't believe they're finally alone, the door locked. The rest of the night stretches away like a sea shimmering with possibility.

It's over all too fast. Jacob doesn't even remember quite how it began, but it hurt. He remembers that much. It hurt a lot and Avery kissed the discomfort away. "Shh," he murmured, kissing Jacob's soft moans from his lips. After a few moments, the pain gave way to intense pleasure—Jacob remembers that. Avery in him, above him, the motion of their bodies rocking the rest of the world away.

Afterwards Jacob clings to Avery with a desperation that frightens him. He buries his face against Avery's chest, hugging his waist in a tight embrace. They lie together on the bed now, the sheets too warm where they wrap around his legs, but he doesn't kick them free.

Avery is tangled around him, too, like the sheets. He holds Jacob close. He's already wiped away the tears that

Jacob cried when they were finished.

Jacob never felt so alone, so afraid and unsure, than he did the moment he felt Avery slip free.

But Avery didn't leave him. Avery held on, smoothing the curls from Jacob's face, kissing the tears that stung his eyes. "It's okay," Avery whispers. "Jacob, it's okay. Don't cry. I love you, it's okay."

Jacob's eyes feel grainy, tired. Everything below his waist is so damn sore. He thinks he'll walk funny for a week. When he crawled out of bed to wash up, he moved gingerly, like a tenderfoot fresh off a horse. In just a pair of boxers, he hobbled through the hall. He hoped he could avoid the other boys on his floor. He's sure they heard his cries when he came, or heard the bed knocking against the wall. He feels as if the whole world knows he's done it now. He doesn't know how he'll keep from blurting it out to his mom when she calls again.

But there was no one else in the hall, just him. In the bathroom, he used the stall instead of the urinal. He wanted to see if he was bleeding.

He wasn't.

That surprises him. He hurts like he should be bleeding. Avery tells him he was, just a little, but it heals up quick down there.

"It'll ache tomorrow," he says once they're back in bed, Jacob in his arms again. His hands rub along Jacob's back in gentle patterns. "God, Jacob. You're amazing. I love you."

Jacob smiles, a little sad. He wishes he hadn't cried. "Love you, too," he whispers. He squeezes Avery tighter. He doesn't know how amazing he is but he's glad Avery said he was.

He doesn't feel amazing, though. What he feels is

empty inside, hollow, used up and tossed away like the condom that sits at the bottom of his trash can now, buried beneath balled up scraps of notebook paper. He wants Avery to fill him up again, make him whole. He stares into the darkness around them and sighs. Avery turned out the light a while ago, when Jacob went to the bathroom. Now it's late. The hall around them is silent. Jacob feels as if they're the only two who exist anymore. The only two who are real.

Well, he knows Avery is real. He can feel Avery's body, solid alongside his own. He can feel Avery's breath ruffle through his curls. Jacob smells him, tastes him, cuddles into him and holds on as tight as he can.

But the only thing that tells Jacob he's real, too, is the dull pain between his legs, Avery's hands along his skin, the tender kisses Avery keeps dropping onto Jacob's hair and face. Jacob's afraid if Avery falls asleep, those things will stop, even the pain. He doesn't want any of it to stop. He wants this, tonight, forever.

So he sighs. He wants to talk. "Was it like this for you?" He means the pain. He means the cuddling afterwards. He doesn't want to picture Avery in someone else's arms, but he has to ask. He has to know.

Avery shrugs. It's an easy movement that settles them closer together, like pieces of a puzzle fitting into place. "Not really." When he talks, his voice rumbles through his chest and into Jacob.

Jacob loves the way it rolls through him like thunder.

"No?" Jacob raises his head to rest his chin against Avery's chest. He looks up at Avery's neck. It curves, graceful, in the faint moonlight. "Why not?"

With a sigh, Avery admits, "We were drunk. Well, Greg was, anyway. I was just tipsy. One of the seniors he knew had some alcohol. When we got back to our room, he started kissing me, telling me how much he wanted me. You know, all that shit you want to hear."

Jacob nods. He knows. He loves to hear Avery say it, but that's different. He knows Avery means it. He thinks this Greg kid probably said it to anyone once he had a few beers in him. Wasn't Greg caught in the showers with another boy? Jacob remembers Avery telling him that.

Another sigh. Jacob suspects Avery doesn't want to ruin tonight with the memory of his own first time. He's sorry he brought it up. But when he starts to say it's okay, Avery doesn't have to answer if he doesn't want to, Avery says, "He wasn't… he was Greg. I know you don't know what that means, but it's hard to explain. It wasn't his first time. Hell, for all I know I wasn't even his first that night, you know? So he wasn't—"

"Like you," Jacob interrupts. "I know I said it hurt, and it did, but I know you went as slow as you could. I know you took your time and you're so gentle and I loved it, Avery, even if it did hurt, and I'm sorry, I'm sorry I almost made you stop. I'm sorry—"

"Shh." Avery strokes his curls, his back, calming him. "It's okay. I know it hurts. I tried to take it as easy as I could because it hurts worse if you just rush into it."

Jacob frowns at Avery's nipple, right beside his eye. When he bats his lashes, they tickle the ruddy skin, teasing the nipple erect. "Did Greg rush it?"

"Jesus," Avery says with a shaky laugh. "It hurt like a bitch."

"And then?" Jacob tightens his arms around Avery. He wishes he could take the memory away.

For a long moment Avery doesn't answer. Jacob thinks it might be too painful still. He wishes tonight had been a first for both of them. He thinks if he ever meets this Greg, he's going to kick the living shit out of the guy for hurting Avery. How could someone hurt Avery? Jacob can't imagine it.

Finally Avery whispers, "Then he went to sleep. That was it. I went back to my bed and that was it."

Jacob closes his mouth over Avery's nipple. He licks around the tender bud until Avery gasps his name. Jacob hates Greg. He hates Tyrone, too, and anyone who ever made this boy in his arms feel anything less than what they both feel right now, at this moment, together.

"I'm glad we waited," he whispers against Avery's skin. "So we can do this."

Jacob hugs Avery so tight neither of them can breathe. He means the cuddling. He's glad they didn't just jump each other in the library or the confessional or somewhere else on the school grounds. He thought about it many times, ached for it, came close to demanding it once or twice, but Avery always said no. Even though he's not thrilled with the circumstances, Jacob's glad Mike's gone so he and Avery can hold onto each other now. He suspects he wouldn't like the sex much if Avery didn't stay with him afterwards. It was good but not great.

This, though, this lying together and talking low and hearing each other breathe… this is wonderful. He doesn't think he could make it through the night afterwards if Avery wasn't beside him, holding him, keeping him safe.

With the hint of a smile in his voice, Jacob asks, "Can I say I love you again? Are you tired of hearing it yet?"

Avery laughs. "You can say it all you want."

He slips a hand beneath Jacob's chin to raise it up, then leans down and kisses him tenderly. All night that's all he's been, tender and gentle and loving. Jacob doesn't want to imagine anything less. Jacob starts to tremble just picturing Avery in Greg's bed, extracting himself from the covers to return to his own side of the room. In his mind Jacob sees Avery's face by starlight that filters in through open curtains. Jacob sees the frown, the confusion, the need to be held. Jacob hugs him, hoping to push the memory away.

Another kiss, this one lingering. Jacob tastes it even after Avery pulls back. "Every time you say it," he murmurs, his lips feathery against Jacob's own, "I'm going to say it, too. So neither of us forgets."

One more kiss. Avery's lips are sweet and soft and damp. His hands lie across Jacob's back, the fingers entangled in the ends of Jacob 's hair. When Avery rolls Jacob against the mattress, he whispers Jacob's name as if he's in rapture. It's a prayer to save them both. He's so heavy above Jacob, a delicious weight in the darkness. Between them Jacob feels Avery harden again, hungry for more. "I love you."

Chapter 7

In the morning Jacob wakes to tiny kisses in the con-
cave of flesh between his collarbone and shoulder.
Warm hands spread across his stomach, lower. Strong
fingers entangle in the hair at his crotch. Even if Avery
never says 'I love you' again, Jacob knows he does. He
feels it in the curve of his boyfriend's body against his, in
the arms holding him close. He wonders how he managed
to wake up every morning alone before this.

Saturday they skip mass to spend the day in bed. Jacob
can imagine nothing better than to stay forever in Avery's
embrace. He hopes Mike never comes back. That night
when they have sex, it doesn't hurt as much as Jacob
remembers. He suspects that, by tomorrow, it might not
hurt at all.

Then Jacob dreams something's happened to Mike
and he has to stay home the rest of the semester. Nothing
bad—maybe he's just too torn up to come back. Maybe
he can't concentrate on his studies, or he thinks he needs
to stay with his family for a while. Jacob's not sure, but
in the dream Mike calls and tells Jacob he's not returning.
He says Avery can have his half of the room.

The dream's so vivid, Jacob can feel the cold wood

beneath him as he sits on the desk in the hall. He can hear Mike's voice, tinny through the phone. Long distance fills the air between them. When he wakes, there's an instant when he's sure it wasn't a dream but real. He's going to be able to wake up to Avery's arms, his kisses, from now until graduation.

But then Avery shifts beside him, still asleep. It's just a tiny movement but enough to dissolve the dream. Jacob lies in the gray Sunday dawn thinking how nice it would be to share his bed with Avery forever. He imagines them older, out of school and working. He pretends this is their time together, before they have to get out of bed and rush around to get ready for work.

He thinks he'd be working at a record store maybe, and wouldn't have to be in until nine. Avery would be a businessman. When the alarm rings, he'd have to dress in a suit and tie and tame his wild hair. He'd kiss Jacob once at the door, twice, a third time before Jacob would shoo him out so he wouldn't be late.

Jacob loves that image. He thinks it's a wonderful dream, better than the one about Mike not coming back.

But he knows it's just make-believe. It hurts more than the other dream did because he wants it to be real more than he's ever wanted anything in his entire life. He's only sixteen—he knows he hasn't wanted much. But he wants this. He wants Avery. It's not just because Avery's his first, either. Jacob's had enough boys to know what he likes. He likes this one, here, with him now. Jacob wants him.

Jacob watches Avery sleep. In the pale light of dawn, he looks cherubic. His cheeks are pinked and round. His lips are that dark salmon of ripened peaches, kissable, begging to be licked, touched, tasted. His eyelashes flutter as he dreams. Jacob wonders what he sees behind those closed lids.

He wonders if Avery is dreaming about him.

The room brightens as the sun rises. The light takes on a golden hue, the last warm light before winter turns it silvery and cold. November has just begun, and Jacob doesn't want to go home at the end of the month for Thanksgiving. He wants to stay here. Or better yet, he wants to go with Avery, wherever it is Avery calls home. He doesn't know if he can make it that extended weekend alone.

He doesn't want to think about December or the long, dark break between semesters when he won't see Avery every day. They've discussed this before, when they should have been studying. He'll call every night before he goes to sleep just to hear Avery breathe, I love you. It'll be the last thing at the end of each day. When his mom asked what he wanted for Christmas, he had to force himself not to tell her he wanted Avery. Wrapped in ribbons, beneath his tree. He likes that image, too.

But he's not thinking about December yet. And he sure as hell isn't thinking about the new year, or Avery's graduation, or the next year, Jacob's junior year of high school without Avery. He doesn't want to think of that at all. He ignores the college catalogues that clutter Avery's floor. When the reps come to talk with the seniors, lining one wall of the cafeteria during lunches, Jacob glares at them because he knows they've come to take Avery away from him.

Not thinking that, he reminds himself. He snuggles closer to Avery, burrowing his head into Avery's shoulder until he feels his lover's arms tighten around him. Lover. It's such a seductive word, sophisticated, grown-up, adult. They're lovers now. Not just boyfriends, and worlds more than friends. Lovers.

And Avery says he's amazing. Jacob feels his cheeks heat at that. He's glad Avery is still asleep. He thinks Avery is more than amazing. He thinks he's fucking phenomenal. Jacob suspects it doesn't get much better than this.

Avery wakes Sunday morning with the hint of a smile on his lips. "Make love to me," he whispers. Outside, the church bells ring across the silent school grounds. Jacob knows they should get up, get dressed, and go to mass. This will be the second day in a row they've skipped. Not going on Sundays is one of the deadly sins at St. Thomas Aquinas. Fortunately there's an evening mass they can attend.

When Jacob rolls onto his back, though, Avery laughs. Softly, gently. "No," he says, easing between Jacob and the mattress. "My turn. Come on. Don't you want to be on top this time?"

Jacob grins, goofy. "Jesus," he sighs. It's all the answer Avery needs.

This time when they come, it's Avery who holds Jacob tight. He doesn't cry, like Jacob did. Instead, he whispers, "I'm going to pretend you're my first."

Jacob raises his head from Avery's chest and studies him a moment. "Why?" He brushes an eyelash from Avery's cheek..

Avery shrugs. "Just because," he says. "You're everything I thought it should be. I should have waited. God, Jacob—"

"It's okay." Jacob doesn't like the tears glistening in Avery's eyes.

With his thumb he rubs across Avery's eyebrows, first one, then the other. They're high, arched, beautiful. Avery closes his eyes tight. One tear squeezes out between his lashes, which clump together into spikes around the drop. Jacob wipes it away. He kisses Avery's nose, then presses his cheek against Avery's own, the skin hot beneath his

"It's okay, Avery." Trying to lighten the mood, he adds, "At least one of us knows what to do. Can you imagine if we both were virgins?"

Avery laughs as he blinks the tears away.

"We'd still be figuring out how to put the damn condom on."

"It's not that hard, Jacob," Avery says with a sigh. "You're so damn cute."

Jacob rolls his eyes. "I know."

That causes more giggles. He stifles them, pressing his face into the pillow beside Avery's head. "I don't want Mike to come back," Jacob admits. Once the words are spoken, he wishes he could take them back. It's a mean thing to say.

But Avery sighs again, rueful. "Yeah. Maybe he won't."

"He will." Jacob doubts Mike's grades will even drop because of this. If anything, he'll probably lose himself in his classes now.

Jacob resents the fact Mike makes better grades than he does. He hates it because he knows he could make those grades too, if he studied. He doesn't want to study, though. He doesn't want to do anything that involves getting out of this bed.

But he closes his eyes and tells himself maybe Avery is right. Maybe Mike won't come back. Maybe they'll be able to stay like this for the rest of the semester.

He decides he hates the word maybe—too indecisive. He wishes he were twenty-three and on his own. He hopes that when he is, he will still know Avery. He tells himself he will.

Right now, alone together in this bed, he can believe that.

Chapter 8

Monday morning comes too soon. Mike will be back today, Jacob knows it, but he's not sure when. He can feel time rushing away from them as he and Avery hurry to dress. He puts on Avery's jacket by mistake, laughing when he looks in the mirror and sees the word Senior emblazoned above the seal on his breast. He wishes he were a senior. Then they could move in together after graduation, go to the same college, get on with life. He feels that high school is just taking too much time away from him right now. Away from them.

Because they're running late, he forgets about the ring on his finger. He's kept it on all weekend long. He doesn't even feel it anymore. Out in the hall Jacob thinks everyone's staring at them. He hears low laughter, the word queer coughed discreetly behind them. But when he turns around, no one meets his angry gaze. What the hell do these fuckers know, anyway? Nothing. Nothing at all. Avery's hand brushes against his almost accidentally when they walk. It's all he needs to keep in check. He won't lose his temper. He won't let them get to him. He won't.

In mass, he notices the ring. He curses beneath his

breath. He's glad Mike's not beside him. He hates to hear Jacob cuss. Especially in the church, of all places. But he thinks God's heard worse than damn it to hell.

He slips the ring off his finger and into his pocket. He doesn't think anyone has noticed. He glances around, just to be sure.

The boys on either side stare straight ahead at the altar. They don't look at him. Jacob notices they don't sit too close to him, like he's got something they don't want to catch. Yeah, he thinks. I'm lovesick. Watch out. He can't believe how much straight guys flatter themselves. Like he wants to fuck them. He's got a boy. He's got Avery. What the hell does he need anyone else for?

Jacob spies Mike in the hallway between classes. He's standing at his locker. A few freshmen huddle near him, the boys he sits with at lunch. Jacob suspects these are the boys who tease him about his roommate. Mike should just tell them to mind their own damn business. That's what Jacob would do.

He leans against the other side of Mike's locker, away from the freshmen. One of them is that Trevor guy from the second day of classes, the one who got him in trouble for talking shit about Avery. Before he even knew Avery. Jacob can't believe how far things have come between them now. He spent the weekend in Avery's arms! Jesus. He wonders what this Trevor kid would think of that. He tells himself he doesn't fucking care. "Hey, Mike."

Mike glances up at Jacob and smiles quickly. "Jacob." He sounds relieved, as if he's happy to see him. Jacob wonders if he even likes these freshmen very much. "Hi."

175

One of his friends snickers. Jacob glares at Mike. He's decided he's going to do what Avery does and ignore these assholes. Let them say what they want about him. He's not getting kicked out of school, like everyone seems to think he will. He won't let them win.

So instead, he taps his books against his hip. He just wanted to say hi to Mike—he's surprised to see him back so soon, like nothing happened. "How are you doing?" He talks low because he's not asking everyone, just Mike.

Mike shrugs. "Okay." He turns slightly toward Jacob, away from his friends. His eyes are wide, sad. Jacob suspects he's not doing okay at all but he forces a smile, pretending he's fine. Without meeting Jacob's gaze, he adds, "I hear you had a visitor this weekend."

The others aren't supposed to hear it but they do. They erupt into snickers, Trevor and a boy Jacob thinks is named Erik, and another kid Jacob doesn't know. The three freshmen lean on each other, laughing. "Visitor," one of them snorts. That sets them off again.

Jacob feels the blood begin to pound in his temples. These motherfuckers don't know what the fuck they're laughing at. He should give them something to laugh about. He clenches his books in his hand until the wires from his notebook eat into his fingers. "You had to bring it up here," he says. He hopes his voice sounds level. He doesn't think it does.

"I'm sorry." Mike looks sorry, too, with his wounded eyes and tight frown. "I didn't mean—"

"Fuck buddy," one of the freshmen says. Jacob thinks it might be Trevor, he's not sure. They all double over, breathless with laughter.

Jacob's had it. Mike could've waited until after

class. He could have waited until they were alone and then mentioned the extra pillow in their room, Avery's clothes folded on Jacob's bed. But no… no, he had to say something here, in front of his friends. Jacob doesn't care if he didn't mean it or not. He doesn't care if his grandfather just died and he's not thinking right. As far as Jacob's concerned, he's never speaking to Mike again. He's already wondering if he can switch rooms during winter break.

"Jacob," Mike pleads. He closes his eyes and sighs. "You guys, stop it. Jacob—"

"Fuck you," Jacob growls. When Mike reaches out for him, he twists away. Leveling a finger at the trio of freshmen behind his roommate, he announces, "Fuck you all."

The one Jacob doesn't know smirks. "You wish," he mutters.

"That's it." Jacob throws his books down. They hit the floor and fan out into the crowded hall, stopping the flow of students. A sudden hush falls like a shroud around them, silent. Jacob hears his own breath, ragged and loud in his ears. He hears the squeak of a shoe on the battered linoleum when Trevor steps back. He hears a locker slam far away.

Mike's locker creaks as he picks at the metal handle. "Jacob, don't."

"What the fuck did you just say?" Jacob demands. He's looking past Mike at the freshman kid. He's going to hurt someone for that comment.

For a long moment, he stares at the freshmen, Trevor and Erik and the boy whose name he doesn't know. He dares them to say something else, anything at all. One word—that's all he needs. One word and the fight begins.

Trevor looks at his shoes. Erik sniffles, turning away slightly, embarrassed by the attention suddenly focused on him. It feels like the weight of the school presses in on them—Jacob feels it, too. Everyone always stops to watch a fight. It's a rule of high school, and Jacob would be lying if he said he didn't like the audience. He knows they're watching him. He knows he's going to win, and it'll get around that he's not fooling here, and no one will fuck with him again.

The other boy, the one who spoke, glances at the faces around them, waiting, watching, silent. He looks at Jacob, at the books scattered across the floor. Finally the kid shrugs, like he didn't mean anything by his hurtful words earlier. "Nothing," he whispers.

Jacob barely hears the sound over the rush of blood in his ears. "Nothing," he echoes.

Another moment passes. Then the school bell rings. They're late for class.

The students in the hall start to move. They keep a wide berth around the lockers, but Jacob's still waiting. He doesn't think it's over. Then Trevor breaks away from his friends, heading down the hall, and Jacob bends down to gather his books. "Watch it," he snarls as someone's foot narrowly misses his hand. He snatches up his notebook, his clipboard, his English text, stacks them together, and picks them up.

As he stands, he hears a tiny ping where something falls from his pocket to the floor. He has time to look down and see Avery's ring lying on the linoleum. The stone winks up at him.

Avery's ring.

"Oh, shit." Erik laughs, a loud, braying sound that

freezes Jacob in place. When he looks up, he sees the surprise in Erik's face, like he can't believe he's laughing but he can't stop. "You have his ring?" Erik asks. "Jesus, Dan, look at that. Like they're going steady."

Dan leans down and tries to grab the ring. Jacob kicks at him, hard. He feels his foot connect with the kid's chest, and thinks he feels ribs crunch beneath his shoe. Dan grabs his side where Jacob kicked. He cries out as he falls into the hall. "Motherfucker."

"You think that hurts?" Jacob challenges. "I'll show you what fucking hurts."

He kicks him again, in the same spot, and once more before the kid manages to crawl out of reach. "Touch that ring," Jacob dares. He's so ready for a fight. "Come on, asshole. Come on."

"Damn faggot." Erik shoves past Mike and rams Jacob back against the row of lockers, one foot kicking the ring. It goes skittering across the hall to ricochet off the far lockers. Jacob follows it with his eyes and then Erik pushes him again, pinning him to the wall, and he loses sight of it in the crowd. Avery's ring…

Jacob shoves Erik off him. He manages to get away from the locker before the freshman throws him back. "Let me go," he mutters through clenched teeth. He lashes out with his fists, hitting Erik in the chest, the stomach, the face. He kicks the lockers and Erik's legs, fighting like a cornered animal. When Erik's hands pull at his hair, he bends over and drives into him like a quarterback, throwing him across the hall, through the crowd, into the other lockers. Erik's hands entangle with his curls, pulling so hard Jacob's eyes tear. He's sick of this shit, all of it, the sniggers, the fear, the snide remarks and hateful stares and constant comments. And he's so tired of fighting. So damn tired.

His fists pummel into Erik, over and over again. He's sick of it, so fucking sick and tired—he punctuates each thought with another jab. He doesn't see Erik anymore, doesn't feel the body beneath his hands as he hits. When Erik slumps against the lockers, Jacob doesn't notice. He keeps punching, his knuckles scraping open on the metal until they're bloody and raw. He doesn't see the blood through his tears. Most of it isn't even his.

His hands move on their own, keep hitting, keep hurting. He doesn't think he can get them to stop.

Part 4

Chapter 1

Avery is late for his economics test. He knows he should've at least opened the book this weekend but he was too busy with Jacob. He doesn't regret that in the least. He loves that boy, everything about him. This is more than what he thought he felt for Tyrone or Greg. It's more than he's ever felt before. He thinks there will never be anyone like Jacob for him again. He doesn't plan to ever let him go. He's only seventeen—this doesn't seem like such an outrageous idea to him.

He already knows they'll run up the phone bills over winter break. He's applied to several colleges but he's waiting to hear from State. That's where Parker goes. He wants to go there too so he can stay close to Jacob. He's already trying to work out in his mind how they'll spend the summer together. They have to—he's going to make sure they do.

Avery hurries through the halls, notebook open for some last minute cramming, but his thoughts are miles away. He's thinking of summer and Jacob and the beach. Of how that boy will look climbing out of a pool, water beading on his chest, his curls, swim trunks clinging to his ass. Of making love in the water. Or on the sand, the sun beating down on them. He turns the corner, flipping to another page in the notebook. He's going to fail this test, he knows it.

In front of him, a knot of students blocks the hall. Avery starts to push through. He wonders why these kids are still here and not in their classrooms. The bell's already rung. He wonders what's keeping them here, what they're looking at—

Somewhere ahead of him, unseen, someone crashes into the row of lockers and cries out. A fight, Avery thinks, and immediately on the heels of that thought, Jacob. Jesus, no.

Avery shoves his way through the students. They move aside like balloons, effortlessly, easily, in whichever direction he pushes. No one stops him. No one says a word.

When he breaks through the crowd, he sees Jacob. He has a boy pinned to the lockers. His elbows pump, fists striking the kid, the lockers, the air. Avery can hear his breathing, heavy, ragged. As the kid slumps to the floor, Jacob keeps hitting him. It's as if he can't stop.

There's another kid lying on the floor, holding his ribs and taking quick, shallow breaths. He's curled into himself, whimpering. By his head lies a ring. Avery recognizes it at once. Mine.

He scoops up the ring and pockets it. "Jacob," he says. "Jacob, God. Stop it! Jacob—"

He grabs his boyfriend's shoulders to pull him off the other boy. "Jesus, stop it already, will you? Just stop it, please."

Jacob takes a steadying breath. He steps back to stare at the boy, bloodied, at his feet. The kid's lips move as if he's mumbling the rosary, fingers twitching like he's reading the beads. But his eyes are closed, one swollen shut. Avery can't hear what he's saying.

Avery can feel Jacob tremble in his grip. "Oh, fuck," Jacob whispers. He turns to Avery, then looks past him, seeing the crowd for the first time. Then he looks at his hands, splattered with blood.

Avery doesn't know if any of it is Jacob's. It's an uncharitable thought but he prays that it isn't.

"Oh, Christ," Jacob sighs. He's shaking, his hands unsteady. He closes them into fists again just to stop their tremors. "Oh, Avery, what the hell…"

Behind them, the murmurs start.

"Sister Mary—"

"The monsignor's here."

"—Big fucking trouble now."

Avery turns as the crowd starts to move again. He sees the black hoods of nuns parting the students like Moses crossing the Red Sea.

He looks at the students, anger and fear mingled in their haunted eyes. He sees the kids on the floor, crumpled and broken. Jacob did that. Jacob hurt them. Because they hurt him first, he thinks. He's never wanted to hold Jacob more than he does at this instant. He wants to hug him close and kiss away the pain and promise him everything will be all right, even though he knows it won't. They hurt him and no one will see that. They'll just see this, because you can't see his wounds. You can't see the way their words have cut him. Avery knows the fighting was wrong but it probably wasn't Jacob's fault. He squeezes his boyfriend's shoulders, trying to comfort him. He knows it's not his fault. He knows.

Suddenly Mike is there beside him. "He's fucked," he says. The swear word sounds funny, foreign on his lips. Avery frowns at him. "They'll kick him out, you know it. He's—"

"Run," Avery says. He pushes Jacob away from him.

Jacob turns, baffled. For a moment he just stands there, hands held out, bloodied, beseeching. In his eyes, Avery can see his heart break. He doesn't understand what's happening, why Avery is pushing him away. Oh, please, Avery prays. He hopes Jacob can read his love in his face. I can't say the words right now, Jacob, but I love you. Please just run. Run and stay safe. Run...

"Get out of here!" His voice is sharper than he intends, louder. It echoes through the silent hall.

When Jacob doesn't move, Avery shoves him again, harder. "Go on," he hisses. "Get the hell out of here, Jacob."

"Avery," he sobs. Tears streak down his cheeks. "I'm sorry."

It's torture to hear the ache in his voice. Oh, baby, I know. I'm sorry, too. So damn sorry they've done this to you... "Please," Avery whispers. "Jacob, please. Just leave."

He thinks Jacob isn't going to move. But then the nuns are there. They see the blood and the bruises. "My Lord!" one of them cries as she falls to her knees by one of the injured boys. Avery wonders if that's considered blasphemous coming from a woman of the cloth.

But it sets Jacob in motion. "Avery," he whispers, voice strained. Then he turns and runs away.

He's missed his economics test, and his English class, and lunch. Avery thinks he'll miss the rest of his classes, too, and maybe dinner as well. He's been sitting on the bench outside of the monsignor's office for so long now. He suspects they might never let him move again.

The boys Jacob fought were freshmen, friends of Mike's. Students milled around the halls until the ambulance came. After the EMTs loaded the boys onto stretchers and wheeled them away, the nuns threatened suspension for anyone lingering at the scene. They called it that, the scene, like it was the spot of a heinous crime. Avery is surprised no one's broken out the yellow police tape yet.

Avery had to call his parents. He still hears the shock in his mother's voice when he told her she needed to come to the school. "Why?" she asked, over and over again.

"I can't tell you that," he replied. The nun from the monsignor's office, Sister Mary Margaret, watched him too closely. He didn't want to tell his mom what happened over the phone. "When you get here."

"Are you in trouble?" Leave it to Diane Dendritch to cut to the chase. She said the word trouble with an incredulous lilt, like her only son wasn't capable of such nonsense.

"Not me," he whispered. "Not really. Just, Mom— please come. They want you to."

"I'll be there," she told him. When he closed his eyes, he saw her disapproving stare, her disappointed frown. "Don't you say a word to anyone until I get there, do you hear me?"

Avery heard. Even when Mike sits beside him on the bench, waiting for his parents to arrive, Avery doesn't say a word. He doesn't ask Mike what happened—he'll hear that from Jacob himself. He wonders where Jacob is. He's heard the nuns whisper, seen the priests shake their heads. He knows Jacob isn't inside the school building or the dorms. He can't imagine where else he might be.

When Mike's parents arrive, they huddle around their son protectively. His mother glares at Avery, distrustful. "Who's this?" she asks. Her voice is shrill. She talks as if Avery isn't even there.

"Avery," Mike tells them. "Jacob's friend. He's not—"

But his mother isn't listening. She pulls Mike up from the bench, moving her son to the far side of the hall. Mike looks back at him, once, before she blocks him from Avery's view. When the nun says the monsignor will see the Nelsons now, Mike is steered past Avery with a cool efficiency that scares him. He didn't do anything wrong, neither of them did. He has a bad feeling no one will realize this.

Avery stares at his hands, twisting in his lap. He spreads them out to still them and grasps his knees. His fingers tremble from the memory of holding Jacob. Please, he prays. It's an endless mantra in his mind. Please let him be okay. Please, God, please.

The door at the end of the hall opens. A rush of cold air sweeps in, swirling around Avery's feet. He looks up at the short blonde woman who enters. She holds a little boy by one hand and looks around warily. Though he's never met her, Avery knows immediately that this is Jacob's mother—he sees Jacob in her eyes, her smile, her curls. Before he can stop himself he stands, stretching, and walks toward her. "Mrs. Smithson?"

She starts. "Yes?" The boy hides behind one of her legs. He stares up at Avery with wide, frightened eyes. He's a baby Jacob, so adorable. He even has that pout.

Avery remembers his name is Johnny. Where his mother's hand holds his, her fingers are white. "And you are?"

"Avery." He holds out a hand, unsure. He thinks she's going to glare at him like Mike's mother did. If she does, he thinks he might cry. He hadn't realized until he saw her how just much he wants her to like him. "I'm a friend of Jacob's. I don't know…"

To his surprise, she smiles. She switches Johnny from her right hand to her left, then holds out the right one for Avery to shake. He takes it gratefully. "The altar boy," she says. He laughs. Now she frowns, but it's not at him. It's at the sterile hall, the monsignor's closed door. "What's going on?" she asks. "What's he done now?"

"Got into a fight." Avery leads her to the bench, where she sits down. Johnny clambers up into her lap. "I don't know what happened. I just came in at the end. They took two boys to the hospital—"

She covers her mouth with her hand and squeezes her eyes shut. Johnny stares up at Avery in that unashamed way children have around strangers. "My God," Mrs. Smithson whispers. "Jacob—"

"He wasn't one of them," Avery assures her. He sinks to one knee and rests a hand on Johnny's leg. When he smiles at the boy, Johnny smiles back. Yes, that's definitely Jacob's grin.

Her hand falls to her lap, limp. "Where is he?"

Avery hates himself when he has to shrug. "I don't know."

Before he can say more, the door to the monsignor's office opens. The Nelsons file out, father, mother, son. None of them look at him as they pass. Not even Mike.

Sister Mary Margaret comes out into the hall. "Mr. Dendritch?"

187

Avery stands. "My parents aren't here yet."

But the nun stands aside, waiting. "Nice meeting you," Mrs. Smithson says. She touches Avery's hand, pressing her fingers into his palm. Her touch is warm, comforting. "I'm glad he's got someone here. It's hard for him to make friends."

"I like him a lot," Avery tells her. It's the understatement of the year.

"Mr. Dendritch?" the nun prompts again.

This time Avery doesn't argue. He lets her lead the way into the monsignor's office.

Chapter 2

It's warm inside the monsignor's office, unbearably warm. Avery suspects the heat's turned up to the sauna setting. He's surprised there aren't any tropical plants in the corners.

And it's dark. Avery feels as if he's walked into a museum, it's that dimly lit in here. The dark carpet, dark wooden paneling on the walls, dark curtains that block the sunlight. In this room, it's neither night nor day but an indeterminable mix of both. Avery thinks that, in here, time has frozen as hard and as still as the winter ground outside.

"Mr. Dendritch," the monsignor says in his slow drawl. Darth Vader, the students call him behind his back. Avery wonders if he knows that. He motions to the plush chairs in front of his desk, three in all. "Have a seat."

Picking the chair on the end, Avery sinks into it and stares at the folder open on the monsignor's desk. His folder. He can read the last four digits of his Social Security number written on the tab. He's happy to see it's just a slim folder. He hasn't been one of St. Thomas Aquinas' worst.

He toys with a button on his shirt. He sees that the

thread is starting to unravel. He thinks it might fall off soon. He picks at the thread, pulls it a little, then smoothes it back down. He's going to have to sew that back on.

"Mr. Dendritch," the monsignor says again.

Avery looks up, aware he's trying to avoid the priest. It doesn't work. The monsignor watches him steadily through wire-framed glasses with an impenetrable gaze. Avery believes this is the look of the Sphinx when it sat outside Thebes, eternally bored, so sure its riddle would never be solved.

"Yes, sir?" Avery asks. His mom would be proud. He's terrified but remembers his manners.

A shuffle of papers on the desk. The monsignor reads something, sets it aside, and picks up something else. Avery realizes they are copies of the letters of recommendation his teachers wrote for him for college. He wonders what they say.

"I don't believe we've met before, Mr. Dendritch," the monsignor intones. His heavy breathing fills the tiny room. Avery imagines he's on the Death Star, trapped like Princess Leia was in the first Star Wars movie. He remembers the fear in her face when Darth Vader tells her he has ways of making her talk. Avery suspects that same fear is probably on his face right now. "You're not one of the students dispositioned to visit me often, are you?"

"I don't..." Avery isn't sure what the monsignor is asking.

"Your teachers speak highly of you," the priest continues. He looks at Avery over the top of his glasses and frowns until the corners of his mouth disappear on either side of his chin. "You're not a troublemaker. You haven't been in here before. Have you?"

Avery clears his throat. "Actually, sir," he says. He

hates to correct the monsignor but he wants to be honest. "My freshman year. I was suspended for skipping a holy day service. Only once."

The monsignor smiles. It's a cold gesture, humorless. "Lesson learned, eh, Mr. Dendritch?"

Avery nods. "Yes, sir." He doesn't mention that another boyfriend had been the one to get him in trouble that time. And he doesn't mention Greg, whom the monsignor surely remembers. He was always in this office. Fortunately it wasn't Avery he was caught with that last time. So he wasn't the one in trouble then.

The monsignor sets the papers aside. He leans back in his chair. It creaks beneath his weight, groaning in protest as he settles against it. He steeples his fingers over his wide stomach, then fixes Avery with his steady gaze. "So why are you here today, Mr. Dendritch?"

Avery shrugs. "I'm not sure," he whispers. I wasn't there, he wants to add, but he thinks the monsignor must know that by now. He's sure Mike said something already.

The monsignor studies his hands as if he's reading what's written on his palms. "You are friends with this Jacob Smithson, are you not?"

Avery nods. "Yes, sir." He won't deny it.

"Good friends, Mr. Dendritch?" The monsignor glances up at him.

Avery nods again. "The best, sir. He's…" He smiles, thinking of the way it feels to hold Jacob close. "He's not as bad as they say, Father. He's funny and smart and…"

And beautiful and loving and means more to me than anyone else in this whole world. But he doesn't say that.

Instead, he tells the monsignor, "He's lonely, I think. Not used to having people be nice to him, maybe. I don't know. I just know he's great to hang out with, you know? He's made this year fun for me."

You don't know how much fun, he adds silently.

"Mr. Nelson says—" The monsignor stops, catching him with that stare. "His roommate. You know him, as well?"

"In passing," Avery admits. He doesn't know much of Mike, just what Jacob tells him. The kid always seemed nice to him, maybe a little too eager to be friendly but nice all the same. He knows Jacob doesn't like Mike, though. He knows it's because Mike probably has these ideas of what roommates should be—inseparable, sharing long talks after the lights are out, campy shit Jacob doesn't go for. He thinks Mike's just lonely, too. He wishes Jacob had been nicer to Mike.

The monsignor nods and picks up where he left off. "Mr. Nelson tells me that you stayed the weekend in his room."

Oh, Jesus, no, Avery thinks. Suddenly he feels sick, dizzy. He's glad he's sitting down.

If the monsignor notices, he doesn't comment on it. "Mr. Nelson was called home for a funeral and Mr. Smithson asked if you could spend the night with him. Is this correct?"

Avery doesn't think Jacob asked Mike but he nods anyway.

The monsignor continues. "He told me it was because Mr. Smithson has an irrational fear of the dark. He said that he hates to stay by himself during the night."

Avery stares at the priest, confused. Jacob never told him that.

The look on the monsignor's face is hard to read. Does he buy that? Avery can't tell. In his humorless voice, the monsignor tells him, "Mr. Nelson agreed to let you stay in his room because he didn't want his roommate to be afraid by himself. Is this true?"

Avery doesn't know if it is or not, but the monsignor is waiting for a reply so he simply nods again. He doesn't trust himself to speak. Mike told Darth Vader here that Jacob's scared of the dark? He's sixteen, Avery wants to laugh. He wasn't scared of the dark when we were in the confessional getting it on. He wasn't—

His hands go numb. He knows exactly where Jacob's hiding out.

The story, as the monsignor tells it, is that Jacob was in the hall with Mike between classes when a handful of freshmen starting picking on him. "Because he had a friend sleep over," the priest said. Avery can't believe the kids would tease him about that fear of the dark thing. The monsignor's frank stare suggests he doesn't believe it, either. "You know what they say about boys like that, don't you, Avery?"

Avery's hands tremble. He keeps them folded tightly in his lap. He wants to leave here and rush to the chapel. He's so sure Jacob is there, waiting to be found. By him. "Yes, sir," he says. He hopes his voice is steadier than his hands.

"Sometimes kids misinterpret things," the monsignor continues. He's watching Avery carefully, gauging his reactions. Avery hopes his face is as straight and bland as he wants it to be. "Sometimes kids just don't like other kids, and they call them horrible names, accuse them of terrible things, just to inflate their own egos."

Avery nods.

"Mr. Nelson tells me the fight started when these boys called Mr. Smithson… unsavory names. Hurtful names, because you stayed with him over the weekend. Can you imagine what these names might be?"

Avery knows all too well. He's heard them himself, behind his back. Queer and homo and faggot—those are the nice ones. Butt-fucker and cocksucker—those sting worse. He ignores them, telling himself they aren't directed his way. He's found when he doesn't turn around or try to fight back, the kids lose interest in him quickly. They can't pick at a wound that doesn't bleed.

"I'm sure they weren't nice," Avery whispers. He prays to God that the monsignor doesn't make him say the words out loud. "Probably dealing with his, um… sexual preference."

The word sexual stabs the air between them, sharp, baited. Avery feels his cheeks heat up because he said it to a priest, of all people. With a nun present. Jesus.

"Exactly." The monsignor sighs, a weary sound. Avery realizes the man just wants this all to blow over. Two students in the hospital—that can't reflect favorably on the school. When the monsignor speaks again, his voice is strained, tired. "So Mr. Smithson does what any hot-blooded boy his age would do in that situation. He fights back."

Avery nods again. "Yes, sir."

"Which is where you come in." The monsignor leans forward. "Tell me what happened when you showed up."

Avery stares at a spot on the wall behind the monsignor's head. He wonders what Mike said about him. He wonders what the monsignor already knows, what he should tell him now. "Um," he says, thinking. He can't believe that bit about the dark. He thinks Mike might have made it up. If so, the boy deserves more credit than Jacob's ever given him. "I was running late? For my class. I had my book open because I had a test."

That I missed anyway, he thinks. He hopes he can make it up. "When I saw the kids in the hall, I knew it was a fight. But no one was doing anything, you know? No one was trying to break it up. So I stepped in. And it was Jacob. I told him…"

He swallows thickly. "I told him to run," he whispers. "I meant to the bathroom, maybe, because he had blood on his hands and I wanted him to clean up. I didn't want him to get into any more trouble. I just wanted him to calm down. I didn't mean for him to run away."

Quietly, the monsignor asks, "Do you know where he is?"

I didn't, Avery thinks, but now I might have a clue. If you let me leave, I'll find him. I don't want you to find him first. "No," he whispers.

For a long moment, the monsignor stares at him, silent. Avery is so sure his lie is written plainly across his face. His hands twist together in his lap. Just when he's about to confess, say he's sorry but Jacob's in the confessional, he's almost certain of it, the monsignor says, "Well. He's probably afraid."

"Very," Avery agrees. He forces a quick laugh. "I'm afraid, too."

"Of what?" the monsignor wants to know.

"I'm afraid he'll be expelled," Avery admits. "I'm afraid this is going to show up on my transcript." He shrugs. "Stuff like that."

This time when the monsignor smiles, his face softens.

"You've done nothing wrong, Mr. Dendritch. If anything, you're the one who stopped the fight. This little talk won't be reflected in your folder."

"What about Jacob?" Avery leans forward, urgent. "What will happen to him?"

"I'm not at liberty to say," the monsignor tells him. Avery falls back in his chair, defeated. "I've only heard Mr. Nelson's version of the story. There are still the other boys involved. Two will stay at the hospital overnight. That won't reflect favorably on Mr. Smithson, as you can imagine."

"Yeah, I know." Remembering his manners, Avery adds, "Sir."

The monsignor begins to rearrange the papers on his desk, a signal that their little talk is nearing its end. "Mr. Nelson gave me the name of the third freshman at the scene. We need to hear their stories, I'm sure you understand. And we need to find Mr. Smithson. It's doesn't look well for him that he's curiously absent." He glances at Avery. "You may go now. Thank you for your help, Mr. Dendritch. If I have further questions—"

Unable to stop himself, Avery falls to one knee, his hands crossed where he catches the edge of the wooden desk. "Please," he whispers.

The monsignor watches him, his impassive face bemused.

"I don't expect you to understand but he's my friend, Father. I know what he did was wrong but God, he's hurting, too. You have to see that. You have to see he's not like what they say he about him. You have to see..." He trails off. He wants to say, you have to see how wonderful and amazing and breathtaking he is. How can anyone look at Jacob and not see all those things and more?

"Please," Avery says again. He's pleading, and it's undignified, and did he just take the Lord's name in vain? In front of the monsignor, of all people... he hopes not. "Please give him a chance. Please don't send him home."

"I need to talk with him before I make any decisions," the monsignor says. His deep voice is gentle, incongruous with the vile image of Darth Vader stuck in Avery's mind. He pats Avery's hands. "If you find him, tell him that. I can't do anything without speaking with him first."

Avery nods and rises to his feet. The nun opens the door for him. "Yes, sir." His chin trembles. "If I find him."

God, he prays as he leaves, please let me find him.

Chapter 3

Avery's mother is waiting outside.

She sits on the bench with Jacob's mom. When Avery comes out of the monsignor's office, both women look up at him as if startled. Johnny stands between his mother's knees. He's the only one who smiles, waving in that little boy way where he opens and closes his fist. For a moment Avery thinks the women will start talking again, dismissing him entirely. He'd like that.

But then his mother frowns. It's her disapproving frown, the one he knew she would wear when she saw him. "I told you to wait for me," she says. It's her way of saying hello.

Avery sighs. "It's okay." Behind him the door shuts quietly. "I'm not..." The one in trouble, he almost says. But a quick glance at Mrs. Smithson, worry etched into her face, keeps him silent. "It's okay."

"If it's okay," his mother says, "then I wouldn't be here, would I?"

Each word is clipped, short. He thinks she's more scared than mad. She wants him to get into a good school after graduation. She knows he doesn't need this on his transcript.

Squatting beside Johnny, Avery touches the little boy's shoulder. He doesn't look at his mother or Jacob's. Instead, he watches Johnny, who holds out a small toy car toward him. "Is that your car?" He doesn't want to deal with adults now. He wants to be a little kid again and let everyone else take care of this mess.

Johnny nods. "I drove us here." To prove it, he rolls the car down Avery's knee. "Vroom vroom. Where's Jacob?"

"I'm not sure," Avery whispers.

"What happened?" Avery's mother demands. Her foot begins to tap nervously. "If you're in trouble—"

"I'm not." Avery watches the car as Johnny moves it around and around on the highway of his thigh. "I'm the one who broke up the fight."

"That's why you're here?" When he looks up at her, Mrs. Dendritch looks unconvinced. "Who's this Jacob kid?" Her eyes say what her words don't. Is he your boyfriend? He sees that in her gaze.

Even though she doesn't ask, he nods. "My friend," he whispers.

His mother's lips tighten into a thin line, bloodless, white. In her lap, her hands squeeze together until her fingers drain of color, threatening to fall off. She knows what he means by that.

Of course she does. She's his mother. The summer after his freshman year she found him on his bed, staring at the ceiling. He had been thinking about Tyrone. That was his first real boyfriend, the first guy he did anything with, and back then it still hurt that he'd been dumped so easily. Sitting on the edge of his bed, she ran a soothing hand across his brow. "You look sad," she told him. "Like someone broke your heart."

"Someone did," he admitted.

Because he didn't know any girls, and because he went to an all-boys' school, she didn't ask if he liked guys. She didn't ask if he was gay. Instead, she frowned and asked, "Do you want to talk about him?"

Him. God, she was so understanding. Even after the fiasco with Greg, she was wonderful about the whole thing. She didn't cry and ask him why he did this to her. She didn't plead with him to try and like women. The only thing she ever said about the whole thing was that it was probably better if they didn't tell his father. He agreed.

And now he feels awful, because she's judging Jacob on the fight and the fact that she's been called here today. Avery wants to tell her Jacob's not like that, it wasn't his fault, but he can't. Not with Mrs. Smithson here. He doesn't think he should be the one to tell her other boys tease her son because Jacob's dating Avery.

So he spreads his hand out on his knee, a roadblock for Johnny's car. The little boy drives the car into his hand. "Beep beep," he says. When Avery doesn't move right away, he drives the car into him again. The tiny metal bumper is cold against his skin. "Beep—"

Avery moves his hand. The car continues, unhindered. "He's a nice kid," he says softly. He's talking about Jacob.

Mrs. Smithson smiles. She thinks he means Johnny. "Thanks." She ruffles her son's hair.

The boy looks up at his mother, at Avery. "I'm thirsty," he declares.

Avery stands. "Do you want some water?"

Johnny slips his small hand into Avery's. "Yes, please." He puts one finger in his mouth, suddenly shy. The car's wheels press against his cheek because he won't put the toy down.

As Avery leads Johnny to the water fountain across the hall, he hears Mrs. Smithson sigh. "He idolizes Jacob," she says. "He's not a bad boy, you must believe me."

Yes, Avery thinks. You must, Mom. He's not bad at all. He's the best thing that's ever happened to me.

Apologetic, Mrs. Smithson says, "He's just hot tempered. He gets it from his father."

"Does he fight a lot?" Mrs. Dendritch asks.

Avery can feel her gaze on his back. At the water fountain he lifts Johnny up. He holds the little boy under the arms while he drinks.

"He's extremely smart," Mrs. Smithson says, as if that's an answer. Avery thinks that's her excuse. Jacob's bored, so he fights. He's brilliant, so other kids pick on him. Avery wishes that were the truth.

In his arms Johnny begins to struggle. When Avery sets him down, the boy takes Avery's hand again. "Is Jacob okay?"

"I hope so," Avery says. Together they walk back to their mothers. Avery matches his pace with the child's.

"Me too," Johnny says with a nod. "I want him to come home."

Me too, Avery thinks, but his idea of home isn't the Smithson's house. It's somewhere safe, with him. He needs to find Jacob soon. He knows Jacob's waiting for him.

A little while later, the monsignor's door opens again. Sister Mary Margaret steps out, her face impassive. "Mrs. Smithson?"

Jacob's mother rises, taking Johnny's hand in both of hers. "Have you found him?"

Avery leans against the wall beside his mother. When the nun shakes her head, he sighs.

"The monsignor will speak with you now," she says. She ushers Mrs. Smithson and Johnny into the room. The door closes behind them.

Easing onto the bench, Avery picks at the ironed crease in his pants and waits for his mother to say something. Now they're alone—classes ended hours ago, it seems, and the building is silent around them. Distant footsteps echo through the empty halls. He has to press his hand over his knee to keep it from shaking. He wants to leave, go find Jacob, find his boy and tell him everything will be okay, even if it isn't right now. He wants to make sure Jacob knows Avery still loves him.

Finally Mrs. Dendritch clears her throat. "How long have you known him?" She's talking about Jacob.

"Since school started." He remembers that first day, the way Jacob's curls shone in the candlelit nave of the church. He remembers the mischief he saw sparkle in those sea-spray eyes. The angels etched into the stained glass windows of the cathedral have nothing on his beauty. "He's not bad, Mom. I really think you'd like him."

"Why didn't you mention him before?" she wants to know.

He shrugs. He's not sure why he never brought Jacob up. Maybe because there was a part of him that wasn't sure what they had between them was real. It was so sudden, an instant attraction that swept them both into a whirlwind that threatens to consume them completely now. Jacob was destined for him. Avery can't imagine it happening any other way. "I don't know." He doesn't

J. Tomas

look at her. He's lost in thoughts of his boy and his flesh and his smile.

His mother touches his hand, then waits until he raises his head to meet her gaze. What he sees in her eyes makes him want to cry. The anger is gone. The fear, gone. This is the woman who used to calm him when he had bad dreams. The woman who picked him up when he fell. The woman who loves him no matter what he does, who he is. When she says his name, he chokes back sudden tears. "Avery, do you love him?"

"God." He closes his eyes, pressing his fingers against his eyelids so the tears don't fall.

"Do you?" she persists.

He nods. "More than anything," he whispers. "I love him, Mom. I do."

Carefully, as if he isn't aware of the situation, she says, "He put two boys in the hospital, honey. Don't you think maybe—"

Avery sighs. "It's not his fault, Mom. You have to believe me." He looks up at her, a tear slipping down his cheek. He wipes it away angrily. "They started it! They pick on him about me and what's he supposed to do? He's not the type to turn away. He was fighting for me."

Until he says the words, he doesn't realize how exhilarating that thought is. Jacob fought for him. Because Jacob loved him. Because Jacob loves him. "You know how boys are, Mom. You know what they say…"

He lets his voice trail off, lets her think about what it is kids say. He hopes she's remembering the time he came home from junior high with a black eye and cut lip because someone called him a 'queerbo' on the school bus. He hopes she's thinking about when his P.E. teacher called to tell her that someone had wrapped his head in a

203

towel and held him under the shower while another kid tried to flush his clothes down the toilet. All because they thought he was looking at them in that way. He hopes she remembers the reason she sent him to St. Thomas Aquinas in the first place—because she thought a private school would be less traumatic, more structured, and safer for her only son.

When she sighs, he knows she's thinking all those things and more. He suspects that now she's going to lecture him on being discreet. He'll apologize for staying the weekend in Jacob's room, even though he loved every minute of it. He's not even sure if she knows about that, but he thinks she might. She's his mother—she knows everything. He'll swear it won't happen again and he'll promise to keep things quiet between them but it's so hard when Jacob's all he can think about. And Jacob's not exactly the silent type. But if she starts in on him, he'll tell her they will try to keep their relationship a secret. As if the whole school doesn't already know.

But she surprises him when she asks, "Do you know where he is?"

Avery wipes his eyes with his sleeve. "I think I might have an idea." He speaks slowly, still waiting for the lecture.

It never comes. When she speaks, her voice is soft, motherly. Her hand squeezes his in a comforting gesture. "Then go find him."

Avery stares at her, dumbfounded.

She forces a smile for his sake. "Make sure he's okay and bring him back here so I can meet him. If he's as wonderful as you say—"

"He is," Avery tells her. Oh, God, he is.

"Then he needs you now," she says. "Find him."

Chapter 4

A very races up the steps of the church but when he rushes into the vestibule, his feet falter. The church is as deserted as the school building, now that classes are out for the day. A heavy pall of incense hangs in the air, suffocating, cloying. The vestibule is dark and musty. Through the open doors ahead, the nave shimmers in a myriad of colors from the setting sunlight cast through the stained glass windows.

Reverently, Avery dips his fingers into the holy water font. The water is as cold as metal against his skin. He crosses himself quickly, dropping to one knee the way he's seen other students do. Genuflection, he thinks it's called. When he looks up, he can see the carved face of Christ staring at him from the other side of the altar. The crucifix. Please, he prays. One word. It sums up everything he hopes and fears.

He takes the side corridor, past the bathrooms. A quick glance behind assures him that he's alone. He pushes through the door marked Stairs, then hurries down the steps. His feet echo off the hollow stairs, incredibly loud. It sounds like hooves, as if the four horsemen of the Apocalypse are thudding down these very steps after him.

He fancies he feels labored breath on his neck, hot, drying his sweat. But when he looks, there's nothing there.

Downstairs. The chapel. He leans against the door for a full minute, listening. He hopes the choir isn't practicing tonight. He doesn't hear anything beyond the heavy wood. With his heart pounding in his throat, his temples, he eases the door open.

The chapel is empty, like the rest of the church. Avery closes the door behind him. He looks around at the pews, the altar, the confessionals... "Jacob?"

His voice is low—even if Jacob were here, he wouldn't hear it.

As Avery nears the confessionals, he looks at the three doors, wondering which one Jacob is behind. He thinks of those horrible TV game shows where the contestants get the prize hidden behind one of many doors. But Jacob isn't a prize—he's a very scared boy right now. He thinks the world is against him. Avery just wants to hold him and kiss him and tell him even if it seems that way, one person still loves him. One person cares enough to come after him. Please, he prays again.

He chooses the door where they first came together in a rush of sexual tension and energy and release. He remembers the cool darkness, the feel of Jacob in his mouth, the taste of his boy on his lips. He raises his hand to knock but it falls to the knob instead. The door opens easily enough. As he pushes it in, the light behind him stabs into the darkened confessional. It illuminates a triangle on the floor, battered loafers against the far wall, khaki legs and hands folded between bent knees. Jacob.

Avery slips into the confessional, closing the door behind him. When he throws the latch, the sound is loud in the sudden darkness. He steps into the black room, eyes wide even though he can't see. He holds one hand out in front of him, feeling his way. When he touches soft curls, he smoothes his hand down the side of Jacob's face. The skin is damp with tears. "Jacob—"

"I'm sorry." Jacob's voice trembles. He presses his lips into Avery's palm. "Avery, I'm so sorry. I didn't mean…"

Avery falls to one knee and covers Jacob's lips with his, cutting off his apology. He cradles Jacob's face as he kisses Jacob quiet. He tastes salty tears when Jacob gives in to him, letting his tongue part Jacob's lips as Jacob sighs into Avery's mouth.

"Avery," Jacob sighs. His hands run down Avery's arms and he slides off the bench to the floor. Avery catches him in a rough embrace. "Oh, Jesus, Avery. I'm so dead. I'm so—"

"Shh." Avery sits on the floor and leans back against the wall, Jacob huddled between his legs. Avery holds him as if he wants to sear this press of their bodies into Jacob's memory forever. "It's okay, Jacob. It's going to be all right, do you hear me? Everything's going to be fine."

Then, because he's been dying to say it and because he thinks Jacob needs to hear it, he whispers, "I love you. Oh, God, I love you. I'm not letting them take you from me, do you hear? I'm not letting you go."

Jacob cries.

"I met your mom." Avery keeps his voice low because it's dark. Jacob still clings to him. Avery has never felt this close, this intimate, with anyone, not even after sex. It's the oppressive scent of the church that does it, he thinks. It makes the confessional so small, so private. It's a place where secrets can be whispered and kept. A place for forgiveness.

"She's here?" Jacob asks.

Avery nods, his chin in Jacob's curls.

Jacob's arms tighten around him. "Fuck. They're going to expel me. You know that."

"Maybe not." But Avery doesn't believe that. The monsignor is waiting for Jacob and he'll talk to Jacob like he promised, yes, but Avery still thinks Jacob will be expelled.

God, he doesn't want that.

So he offers, "Maybe you'll just be suspended for a little bit." Even though he doubts it.

Jacob sighs. The sound breaks Avery's heart. "I'm scared you'll forget me."

"Jacob—"

"I'll be sent home and you'll find someone new," Jacob says over him.

Avery shakes his head. "No. I'll call you every night. Every morning, too. I won't forget you."

Jacob sighs again. "You say that now and maybe you will call at first, but one night I'll sit by the phone and wait and wait and it'll never ring."

Avery shakes his head, denying it. He doesn't think he could ever forget this boy in his arms, even if he tried. "No, you're wrong."

But Jacob continues. "And you'll forget. You'll move on, and maybe I will, too. And God, Avery, I don't want that to happen. I don't want to lose you."

"You won't." Avery hugs Jacob harder, as if to prove to him he'd never let go.

"But if I get kicked out," Jacob reasons, "we'll never see each other again."

"I'll have Parker drive me to your house," Avery promises. "Every weekend. Your mom will get sick of me but I don't care. Or I'll come by and pick you up to bring you back here." He forces a laugh. "You're not getting rid of me that easily."

Jacob buries his head against Avery's chest. Another sigh, this one long and drawn out. "I'm so afraid this is it." His breath is warm through Avery's shirt. "Tell me this can't be it."

"It's not," Avery tells him. He pulls Jacob back and leans down until their noses touch. This close, he can see Jacob's eyes despite the darkness, shiny with tears. "Listen to me—"

"Avery." Jacob holds onto Avery's wrists. He closes his eyes, his face crumpling. Twin tears course down his cheeks.

"Listen," Avery says. His fingers lace behind Jacob's neck. He kisses Jacob, holding his lips to Jacob's as if he can make everything better with that kiss. When he speaks, his mouth moves against Jacob's, and when he licks his lips, he tastes salty tears. "You've got to go back, Jacob. You can't just hide out here forever. You have to be strong."

"I can't," Jacob says. "Jesus, Avery, I can't."

Avery presses his lips to Jacob's forehead. "You can. You're strong enough to stand up for me when those boys started picking on you. You're strong enough to know what you want—"

"You," Jacob whispers. He's crying again. Avery wishes his kisses were enough to stop the tears. "All I want is you, Avery. I'm not going to let them take you away." He lets Avery pull him into his embrace. "I just don't know what to do."

"Listen to me," Avery tells him. Jacob sniffles but says nothing, waiting, listening.

Avery doesn't speak. Instead, he lets the silence fill in all that he wants to say. He lets his arms tell Jacob what his words can't, his hands caressing his lover's curls, his lips soft against his boyfriend's neck.

Beneath his touch, Jacob begins to calm down. His own hands start to feel their way across Avery's thighs, his chest. His heart beats against Avery's own, and his breath evens out.

When the tears are gone, Avery breathes, "I love you, Jacob."

"Avery," Jacob sighs. "I love you, too. I love you so much…" His voice trails off, as if the words can't possibly hold in all the emotion, all the love, everything he feels. "I'm so sorry."

"It's not your fault," Avery reminds him. "You have to tell the monsignor that. It's going to be hard."

"It is," Jacob agrees.

"But remember I'm waiting for you," Avery continues. "Remember I love you. Okay? I'm here for you and I love you and no matter what happens, I'm not going to give you up."

Jacob sighs. "If I get expelled—"

"We'll find a way to be together," Avery promises. "I swear, Jacob. No matter what happens, they can't take this from us. They can't. They aren't strong enough. Do you hear me?" Jacob nods. "They can't tear us apart. We won't let them."

Jacob hugs him, hard. It's all Avery needs to assure himself they can get through this thing. Together.

Chapter 5

Before they leave the chapel, Avery takes Jacob's hand in his. He reaches into his pocket, extracts his ring, and slips it onto Jacob's finger again. "You lost this," he says.

Jacob's eyes fill with fresh tears. He wipes at them roughly with the sleeve of his blazer. "Maybe I shouldn't…"

Avery looks at him sharply. His blood runs cold at the halfhearted protest. "Shouldn't what?"

Jacob shrugs. "If I have to leave, you'll want it back." He doesn't meet Avery's eyes. Instead, he looks at the ring, his chin trembling as if he doesn't want to cry anymore. "I don't think I can do that, Avery. I don't think I have it in me to give it back to you. I'd rather…" He presses his lips together and covers his eyes with one hand. "I'm not that strong."

"I'm not asking for it back," Avery tells him, "not ever. It's yours because I love you. Nothing's going to change that."

He wants to say more. He wants to say the ring is a circle, never-ending, round and round forever. He wants to say that's how his love is, that never-ending, that forever. But he doesn't want it to sound cheesy. It's bad enough they're standing at the end of the aisle, alone in the chapel, Jacob's hand in his as if they're getting married. In his mind it sounds grand, all he wants to say, but he knows that words will only sully his thoughts and debase his emotions. Words will never encompass all he feels for Jacob.

So he kisses Jacob, tenderly, softly. Everything he feels is in that kiss, everything he hopes and dreams and fears. Jacob's hands tremble in his. He squeezes Avery's fingers tightly to still them. "Okay," he sighs. He leans his temple against Avery's, takes a steadying breath. "I can do this."

"You can," Avery assures him. He pulls Jacob into a quick, strong hug. "Come on."

"Mom?"

She stands by the bench outside the monsignor's office, arms crossed, hands cupped around her elbows in a protective, frightened stance. She's reading an announcement taped to the wall and turns when Avery calls for her. He forces a smile, reaching behind him for Jacob. He feels his lover's hand slip into his. Avery pulls him close. One hand eases around Jacob's waist to rest in the small of his back. "This is Jacob."

"Jacob." His mother looks at the tousled curls, the sad eyes, the smile that could make angels weep. Avery holds his breath.

"Hello, Mrs. Dendritch." Jacob's voice breaks as if he's scared. Avery knows he is—he can feel Jacob's body hum beneath his touch. "I'm sorry about all of this..."

Finally she smiles, a little sad herself. "Me, too," she tells him. "It's not the best way to make a first impression."

Jacob laughs at that. "No, it's not."

"Well." Mrs. Dendritch takes a deep breath that she lets out slowly. Avery can tell she's trying to see Jacob the way Avery sees him. She's trying for his sake. He's never loved her more than he does at this moment. "I guess that just means you're going to have to visit us over winter break. So we can get to know each other better. What do you say?"

Jacob's grin lights up his eyes, and his fingers tighten around Avery's own. "I'd love to," he breathes.

"Is my mom still inside?" Jacob rests a hand against the monsignor's closed door as if he's afraid to knock.

Mrs. Dendritch nods. "I think you should be in there, too." She looks at Avery when she says it.

"Yeah," Avery says, though he doesn't want Jacob to leave him. Once Jacob is in that office, Avery has an irrational fear that he'll never see his boy again. But his mother's right. Jacob needs to be in there, listening to what they say about him. He needs to have a chance to tell his story.

Before he can stop himself, he reaches past Jacob and raps on the door. The sound is hard and echoes through the wood. When the door opens, he guides Jacob inside.

Mrs. Smithson sits in the chair where Avery sat when he spoke with the monsignor. Johnny sits on the floor, rolling his car around in circles on the carpet by his mother's feet. The monsignor is still at his desk, a Jedi Knight in his priestly garb. He looks up over his glasses as the two boys enter. "Mr. Smithson," he says in his breathy Darth Vader drawl. If he's surprised to see Jacob, he doesn't show it. "I see Mr. Dendritch has found you. I assumed he would."

Johnny looks up from his car. "Jacob!" He scrambles to his feet and runs across the room right into Jacob's legs. He hugs his brother. "Mommy said we were coming to see you but you weren't here."

"I'm here now." Jacob lifts Johnny up into his arms, grunting because the boy is heavy.

The little boy wraps his arms around Jacob's neck and his legs around Jacob's waist. He smiles at Avery over Jacob's shoulder. "Hi," he says with that open-close wave of his.

"Hi," Avery says back. He leans close, whispering into Jacob's ear. "Remember I'm waiting out here for you."

Johnny giggles. He presses a tiny finger into Avery's cheek, pulling the skin taut into a lopsided grin. "Wait for me, too."

Avery ruffles the boy's hair. "I will," he promises. When Sister Mary Margaret detaches herself from the far side of the room, Avery smiles at Mrs. Smithson before closing the door.

He doesn't like that Jacob's on the other side of it. He wishes he could be in there, too.

Avery sits on the edge of the bench, elbows on his thighs, hands folded between his knees. How long has Jacob been in the monsignor's office? He doesn't know. Too long, that's for sure. "What time is it?"

Beside him, his mother sighs. "Honey, relax." She rubs his bunched shoulders as if she could rub away the tension in his muscles. She can't.

"Mom," he starts, but he doesn't know what else to say so he stops. He feels impotent, useless. He hates this feeling.

After a little while, his mom laughs. It's a small sound, forced for his sake. "He's very cute," she says. She has to be talking about Jacob.

Thinking of him brings a smile to Avery's face. "He is." He rests his chin in one hand and sighs. "Do you really think he can come visit over the break?"

"Sure," she says. "Why not?"

Avery shrugs. "Even if he…" He doesn't want to say what he's thinking. Even if he gets expelled? If he says the words, they might become reality, and he doesn't want that to happen.

But his mom asks, "What's the worse that can happen?"

Another sigh. "They kick him out." He can think of nothing worse than that.

"He only lives an hour away."

Avery closes his eyes. Leave it to his mother to reason things out. An hour is a lifetime away for him, can't she see that? He doesn't have a car. He doesn't think Parker will want to cart him to Jacob's place and back every single time he wants to see his boy.

"That's too far," Avery tells her. "I want him here with me."

"You can't always have what you want," she says. That's a Mom-ism if he ever heard one. She's full of quips like that. Things he feels he should know, things he does know, things that are supposed to make him feel better but don't. "What about next year? If he does stay, you won't be here. What happens then?"

"I'll still be close by," Avery says. "I'm going to go to State."

She sighs. "You don't know that. Have you heard from them yet?"

"No." Avery throws himself back against the bench, angry. "What am I supposed to do, Mom? I don't want to lose him. I don't want…" He sighs. He hates this. In a petulant, childish voice, he says, "I don't want things to change."

Now she laughs again. "How old are you again?"

He pouts at that.

"Things change, Avery. It's part of growing up. If you want to keep what you have with him, you have to work at it. If it's not meant to be, then there's nothing you can do to hold on to it."

"Gee, thanks," he mutters. That's not what he wants to hear.

Mrs. Dendritch continues, uninterrupted. "But if this is it, honey—if this is it, then nothing will be able to keep you two apart." She waits for him to digest this. "You know that. Don't you?"

He lets out a breath he doesn't know he's been holding. "Yeah, but—"

She's not through. "Say he gets expelled. He lives an hour from here. You can talk on the phone. You can visit—"

"Not often," Avery reminds her.

"No," she concedes, "not often, but enough. And he's still welcome to visit any time you're home. He's not that far away."

He looks up at her. He's not really sure where Jacob lives but he knows it's far enough from the school that he can't simply walk there. Didn't his mother say it was an hour away? How does she know? Mrs. Smithson told her, he thinks. That's what they were probably talking about while he was in with the monsignor. He's almost sure of it. "What do you mean?"

She smiles in that way she has that tells him everything's going to be all right. He's always loved that smile. It makes him feel safe and loved. "They only live twenty minutes from the house. You can visit him whenever you want once you get your graduation present—"

His eyes go wide. "A car?" That changes things. If he has a car, he can visit Jacob without asking anyone else to tag along. They can make love in the back seat and hold hands while he drives and… the possibilities are endless. A car. He can't wait to take his boy out in his car. His car. His. "You guys are buying me a car?"

His mom laughs because she knows he's a million miles away right this second. She touches his hand to bring him back. "Don't let your dad know I told you," she warns. "He wants it to be a surprise."

"Oh, it is," Avery assures her.

A car. He doesn't know what kind it is but he pictures Jacob in the passenger seat. He imagines Jacob smiling at him as they drive. The windows down. The wind in his curls. God. He can't wait for graduation now.

Chapter 6

Just when Avery begins to wonder if Jacob will ever come out, the monsignor's door opens. Jacob steps out first, Johnny holding his hand. Mrs. Smithson follows behind her sons. She looks exhausted. Avery and his mother rise to their feet. "Well?" He looks from Jacob to Mrs. Smithson and back again. "What happened?"

Before Jacob can answer, Johnny tugs on his hand. "Bathroom," he declares, looking up at his brother. "You promised. You said you'd take me when we got out."

"Come on," Jacob says. His voice is so soft, Avery can barely hear it. "Take his hand, Johnny."

Johnny's little fingers slip into Avery's palm. With a glance at his mom that says he'll be right back, he lets Johnny pull him along after them. "Jacob?" he asks once they're out of earshot. "What did he say?"

Jacob leads them into the bathroom down the hall. He holds a stall open for Johnny. Avery leans against the wall by the hand dryers, waiting. He's dying to know what the monsignor told Jacob. From his lover's frown, he's guessing it isn't good. "Hold it," Johnny tells Jacob, pushing on the door to the stall to close it. "Hold it tight."

218

Jacob holds the top of the door to keep it shut. "Hurry up, Johnny." He smiles at Avery.

"So are you going to tell me what happened?" Avery asks. "Or do I have to guess?" When Jacob doesn't answer immediately, Avery prompts, "You got kicked out."

"What?" Jacob shakes his head. "No. I mean, not yet. I mean…" He sighs, exasperated. Avery smiles at the way he rolls his eyes. "Do you even know how the whole thing started?"

Avery shakes his head. "Not really," he admits. "I'm thinking someone called you a fag and the rest is history."

"Mike goes, 'I heard you had a visitor this weekend.'" Beneath Jacob's hand, the stall door shakes. He holds it tighter, keeping it closed. "Like these jerks he hangs with won't hear him. So they start laughing, right?"

On the other side of the stall, the toilet flushes. Then Johnny asks, "Jacob? Let me out."

Jacob doesn't hear him. Avery sees his anger returning again, just thinking about what happened this afternoon. "Jacob." He points at the stall.

"So I get all pissed off," Jacob says, ignoring him, "and I throw my books down, ready to fight. I was like, come on, assholes. I'll give you something to fucking laugh at."

"Jacob?" Johnny's hand snakes out from beneath the stall door. He pokes at Jacob's leg, then tugs on his pants. "Let me out, Jacob. I'm done."

"Jacob," Avery tells him, pushing away from the wall. "Your brother…"

Jacob lets go of the stall door. It swings open. Johnny glares at Jacob as he steps out. "You locked me in," he says. He sounds so petulant, Avery laughs. Jacob follows

Johnny to the sink, leaning over him to turn on the water. Johnny shoves his hands under the faucet. When Jacob fills his own hands with liquid soap, Johnny splashes water up at him.

"Hey!" Jacob cries. He takes Johnny's hands in his and soaps them up. "Stop it."

"When did you lose the ring?" Avery watches Johnny lean back against Jacob's chest as he rinses their hands.

"It was in my pocket," Jacob explains. "I forgot to take it off this morning, we were in such a rush. When I knelt down to pick up my books, it fell on the floor." He throws Avery a hateful look. Avery can see why the boys backed down the first time, if Jacob looked at them like that. "That's when the fight broke out."

Avery smiles, hoping to dispel Jacob's anger. "You mean, that's when you kicked their asses."

Jacob laughs. "Yeah." He turns off the faucet and leads Johnny to the hand dryers. As he hits the button to turn on the air, he raises his voice. Johnny steps beneath the dryer, hands held high. The air blows his hair back and dries his hands. "Mike didn't tell Darth Vader about the ring. He said I was afraid of the dark. That's why I had you sleep over. I was like, what the fuck?"

Johnny turns the dryer onto Jacob. "What the fuck?" he mimics.

"Johnny, don't." Jacob turns the dryer back down, slapping his brother's hands away. "Don't say 'fuck.' Mom will kill me."

Grinning up at Avery, Johnny says, "Okay. I won't say 'fuck.'"

"Johnny!" Jacob smacks his shoulder. When the dryer turns off, Johnny hits the button, turning it back on again.

Avery raises his voice over the whir of the dryer. "So, now what?"

Jacob sighs. "Now I'm on probation." He leans against the wall, watching Avery over the top of the dryer. "Three days suspension until they figure out what to do."

"What do you think they'll do?" Avery asks. Three days. He doesn't know how they'll be able to wait that long for the verdict.

With a shrug, Jacob says, "I'm not sure. My mom got evil on them, though. You should've seen it." He grins and ducks his head in that embarrassed way he has that makes Avery's heart skip a beat. "She says everything bad about me comes from my dad's side of the family, but she has her moments."

"What did she say?" Avery can't picture the petite, blonde Mrs. Smithson getting evil on anyone, let alone the monsignor.

"She says she pays a pretty penny for me to go here." Jacob picks at the label on the dryer that's begun to peel. When it turns off again, Johnny turns it back on a third time. He stands beneath the rush of air, giggling. Avery suspects his hands are dry by now. "She says she expects her son to be treated with respect. If kids here can't be disciplined enough to keep away from me, then that's not my fault. She told him it was the school's fault, for allowing bullies in its halls."

Avery laughs. "She didn't?"

Jacob nods. His cheeks flush with pride. When he looks at Avery, his eyes sparkle merrily. Avery loves that look on him. "She says if I get expelled and nothing happens to the other boys involved, then she's going to press charges. I don't know if she can do that or not—"

"You're the one who hit them," Avery points out.

"I know, right? But she also said she's going to the paper about it," Jacob continues. "She will, too. She has a friend who writes one of the columns. She said an exposé on the injustices of a Catholic high school will make the front pages."

Avery doesn't know about that, but he can see where the monsignor would reconsider his decision with that threat hanging over his head. He knows the school's low on funding as it is. That's why Jacob can go here when he isn't even Catholic. As long as his tuition's paid, no one cares what religion he is.

"So," he says. "Three days."

Jacob nods. The dryer cuts off again. When Johnny reaches for the button, though, Jacob takes his hand. "No," he says. "No more. You've had your fun."

"My hands are still wet," Johnny protests.

"They are not." Jacob waits until Johnny stops struggling in his arms before he says, "Three days. What's it like to be suspended here?"

Avery thinks back to the one day he spent in suspension. "Boring," he says. "Like purgatory. You just sit in this room and wait for the day to be over with so you can get out."

"Doesn't sound too bad," Jacob says. "I'll spend the whole day thinking about you."

Avery laughs. "You have to do schoolwork, silly." When Johnny wriggles out of Jacob's grip, Avery takes Jacob's wrist and pulls him closer. "You have a shitload of work, too. The nuns really pile it on. You'll be dead after three days."

"Maybe it'll bring my grades up a bit." Jacob runs a hand beneath Avery's blazer and around his waist. "At least I'll have to study then."

"Yeah." Avery feels something push against his leg. He looks down to find Johnny squeezing between them, pushing them apart.

"Jacob." Johnny tugs on Jacob's arm until his hand falls from Avery's waist. "It's time to go. Mommy's calling us."

With a grin, Jacob says, "I don't hear her." He winks at Avery.

"I do." Johnny pries Avery's fingers off Jacob's wrist. "She says hurry up. Come on."

"I think someone's jealous," Avery says. When he ruffles Johnny's hair, the little boy glares up at him, frowning.

"I think someone has to mind his own business." Jacob covers Johnny's eyes with one hand. As his brother tries to pry his hand away, he kisses Avery. His lips are sweet, tender.

The kiss makes Avery ache for another. Before Jacob can pull away, Avery catches his chin in his hand and claims another kiss. "It should be all right," Jacob whispers. "At least I have three days, you know? At least I don't have to go home tonight."

Avery kisses him once more. This time he eases Jacob's lips apart, slipping his tongue into the damp warmth of his mouth. Between them, Johnny says, "You guys better not be kissing. Let me go, Jacob! I'm going to tell Mommy if you don't let me go."

Avery covers Johnny's mouth with his hand, stopping the boy's words in mid-sentence. Then he kisses Jacob again. These will be the longest three days of his life.

Chapter 7

Before she leaves, Avery's mother tells him to be careful. "Don't let him get you in trouble."

They're outside of the school building now. It's that gloaming time of day when it's just beginning to darken. The halogen lights illuminating the sidewalks hold up the night sky that hangs over the campus like a tent of netting. Here and there a few stars peek through, and the moon hugs the horizon as if too frightened to rise. In the glow of the overheads, Avery thinks his mom looks much older than she should. He wonders if she thinks the same of him in this lighting. He feels old. He feels ancient.

"He's not that type," Avery tells her again. When he kisses her cheek, her skin feels soft and powdery, an old woman's flesh. It makes him sad to think of her like that.

Behind them, Jacob stands with his own mom, Johnny in hand. Johnny wants to see where his brother lives so they're going to take the little boy up to Jacob's room before Mrs. Smithson leaves. From the way Jacob watches the Dendritches, Avery suspects Jacob heard his mother's words. He flashes Jacob a quick grin to reassure him that everything's okay. Jacob glowers a moment longer, then smiles back.

"You invite him over," Mrs. Dendritch is saying. Avery turns toward her, nods. "Over the break—I want to get to know him better."

"Don't tell Dad," Avery cautions.

His mother gives him her patented now, would I do that? look—wry grin, narrowed eyes. A hand on her hip would complete the image. "Don't worry, I won't."

He watches her walk away. When she gets to the gate, she turns back and waves. It saddens him that he didn't tell her about Jacob before today. He tries to remember when he last called her and can't. His freshman year he was always on the phone to her. Now he's a senior, he's growing up. He tells himself he'll call before he has to go home for Thanksgiving. He suspects he'll forget.

On the way to Jacob's dorm, Johnny takes his hand again. The toy car is wedged in the boy's small fingers, pressed into Avery's palm. Avery imagines the little boy wants to stay between the two of them. He holds both their hands.

When Avery leans over to talk to Jacob, Johnny pushes against him, keeping them apart. "Your brother doesn't like me," he says with a laugh.

"Johnny," Mrs. Smithson admonishes. She walks on the other side of Jacob, a distracted look on her face. "Be nice or we'll go home now."

"I want to see Jacob's bed," Johnny declares.

"Then be nice," his mother says again. Her voice is curt, strained. Avery can easily see her using that tone on the monsignor.

Up the stairs to Jacob's floor. The hall is empty, most of the doors closed. Everyone's studying or at the cafeteria for dinner. Jacob leads the way to his door and fumbles with his keys to unlock it, but Johnny shakes free from Avery's hand and turns the knob. It opens easily.

Inside the room Mike sits at his desk, hunched over his homework, as if nothing happened earlier. His parents are gone. He looks up as they enter the room. Johnny hugs Jacob's leg, suddenly shy again. "Mom," Jacob says, waving a hand in Mike's general direction. "That's my roommate. Mike, my mom, my brother." Avery raises his eyebrows at Mike, bemused.

Johnny extracts himself from Jacob and holds his toy car out to Mike as he approaches. "Oooh, cool," Mike says, taking the car. He turns it over in his hands. "Is this your car?"

"Yep." Johnny climbs up into Mike's lap uninvited. He points at the papers strewn in front of him. "What's this?"

"Johnny," Mrs. Smithson warns. She stands near the door, frowning at Avery's clothes folded on Jacob's bed.

"It's okay," Mike tells her. "I have a brother, too. His name's Kevin." To Johnny, he asks, "What's your name?"

Johnny ignores him. "What's this?" He picks up Mike's pencil and starts to draw in the margins of Mike's math book.

Avery smiles at Jacob. If only they would all disappear, he wants to say, making a joke out of it. After all the drama today he only wants to lie down beside Jacob, hold him close, fall asleep with his boy in his arms, and he can't. He hates that.

But Jacob's not looking at him. Jacob's staring at the table by his bed. Avery follows his gaze. The box of condoms sits right beside Jacob's lamp. Open. Obviously in use.

Shit.

Avery glances at Mrs. Smithson, who hugs herself as she looks around the room, a slight frown on her face as if she thinks the whole place needs a good scrubbing. As nonchalant as he can, he begins gathering up his clothes, his pillow, his school books. When he's sure she isn't watching him, he slips the condoms into his pillowcase. He wonders if Mike's parents were in the room earlier. He wonders what Mrs. Nelson had to say about this little box of party favors left out in plain sight.

"Damn," he whispers, brushing against Jacob. He touches the small of Jacob's back for a brief instant. Jacob's hand smoothes across his stomach then is gone. "You don't think she saw—"

"No." Jacob laughs, a little shaky. "Hell, no. We wouldn't be alive if she did."

Avery nods. He hopes whenever Jacob tells her about them, she takes it as well as his own mom did, but he's afraid that might not happen. From what he knows of Jacob's family, they aren't very supportive of him. They'd rather pawn him off on a school like St. Thomas Aquinas and hope he turns out all right in the end. That thought makes Avery love him all the more.

"I should go." He hefts his pillow in one hand, his book bag in the other.

The look Jacob gives him is one of pure torture. "Don't," he says. "Not yet."

"We have to go, too," Mrs. Smithson announces. "Come on, Johnny. Say goodbye."

Johnny slides down from Mike's lap. "Goodbye." He waves at Mike with his fist wave, open, closed. Mike hands him his toy car before he runs back to Jacob. Wrapping his arms around his brother's legs, he sighs. "Come home with us, Jacob."

Avery feels his throat swell. He wants a little brother like Johnny. "Soon," Jacob promises. He kneels as he hugs Johnny tight. "I'll come home soon, Johnny. Okay?"

Avery hopes it's not too soon. He hopes it's not because he's expelled.

Jacob stands, taking Johnny's hand in his. "Wait here for me?" he asks Avery. "I'll walk you back."

Avery nods. "Sure."

He sits on the edge of Jacob's bed. Mother and sons file out into the hall, shutting the door behind them. He's alone with Mike now. He smiles at the sophomore then lies back on the bed, waiting for Jacob to return.

Mike breaks the silence first. "So what happened?" He toys with his pencil as he looks over his shoulder at Avery. "Did they kick him out?"

"He's suspended for now." Avery folds his hands behind his head and stares up at the ceiling. He remembers the way the bed creaked beneath their combined weight when they shifted in each other's arms. He wishes Mike was gone so they could be alone when Jacob gets back. Avery wants to make love to him again.

"How long?" Mike asks.

"Three days." Avery knows a lot can happen in three days. Johnny might get his brother home after all by the end of that time.

"And then?" Mike presses.

Avery sighs. "And then they're going to decide what to do. I don't know, Mike. I just don't know."

For a minute neither of them speaks. Avery can hear Mike's eraser scratch along the pages of his book, rubbing away Johnny's pencil drawings. He wonders if Jacob walked his mother all the way to her car. It's taking him long enough to get back.

Finally in a small voice, Mike says, "My mom wants me to switch rooms."

Avery sits up, frowning. "Why?"

Mike shrugs. He's bent over his book again and Avery can barely hear him. "She thinks Jacob's a bad influence. She says he's going to get me into trouble." When Avery doesn't answer, he adds, "She wants to ask the monsignor to move him somewhere else."

Somewhere else. Avery doesn't think there's anyone in the school who will room with Jacob now. Not with the fights, or the rumors. A new roommate might be hateful, root through his stuff, beat him up while he sleeps. God, no, Avery prays. Let Mike find a new room and Jacob stay in this one alone. If he stays at the school at all.

Mike takes a deep breath, then lets it out slowly. "I told her no."

He sits back and turns to face Avery. He looks scared, like he's not used to defying his mother. But he also looks thrilled that he did, surprised he had it in him. "He's the coolest guy I know, Avery. I know we're not, like, best friends but at least he talks to me, you know? As long as we share a room, at least we have something in common."

Avery grins. "You like him, eh?" He laughs at the blush that colors Mike's cheeks.

"Oh, God," Mike says, rolling his eyes. "Not like that. You can't think—"

"I'm teasing," Avery assures him. "If I did think that, I'd have to hurt you. He's my boyfriend."

Mike turns a deeper shade of red. "I so don't need to hear this," he mutters.

Avery laughs again. "You didn't swipe any of my condoms, did you?" He's decided he likes making Mike embarrassed. He makes a show of pulling the box out from his pillowcase. Dumping the contents into his lap, he counts the condoms. Seven, just as there should be. "We only used three—"

"Stop!" Mike turns back to his homework, blushing furiously. "I don't even know why I bother talking to you guys." Avery starts to speak again but Mike covers his ears. "No, I'm not listening. I'm not!"

Avery sobers up. "I'm only kidding." He puts the condoms back in the box, then hides the box in his pillowcase again. "You didn't have to lie for him, you know."

Mike removes his hands from his ears. "I don't want him kicked out," he says. "It's my fault the fight started. I shouldn't have said anything."

No, Avery thinks, you shouldn't have. You should've kept your mouth shut. Instead of saying that, he asks, "Do you mind that I slept over?"

Mike is quiet for a long time. Avery lets him think. He begins to suspect Jacob will return before he answers.

At last Mike shakes his head. "No," he sighs. "Just don't... I don't know, just don't do it when I'm here, okay?"

Avery laughs. "You don't have to worry about that," he promises. Jacob's loud when he comes and Avery doesn't like an audience. He wants those sighs, those moans, those cries all to himself.

Chapter 8

In the morning, Avery meets Jacob outside his dorm, as usual. They sit through mass with their separate classes. It's hard for Avery to keep his thoughts on the service. They keep turning to Jacob, his curls, his smile, the feel of his body in Avery's arms, his skin beneath Avery's hands. He can't wait until the break when Jacob will visit him at home. He's already looking forward to sex in the hammock his mother has set up in their backyard. It's hidden behind his father's tool shed. No one will see them back there.

After mass, Avery walks Jacob to the monsignor's office. He reports there for suspension. On the first day, the other two boys are there, too, already sitting on the bench. Jacob's told Avery their names are Dan and Erik.

Dan holds his side when he walks—his ribs are bruised, not broken, and he wheezes as if he's winded. Erik has a broken nose, stitches above his left eye and below his lower lip, and an ugly welt on his temple. Neither boy looks up as Jacob sits down beside them on the bench.

When classes are over, Avery hurries to the detention hall. It's a short corridor that runs between the monsignor's office and the nurse's station. At the end of the hall is one room. Avery knows the walls are blue inside. Each desk is in a cubby, like in an office, with partitions separating the students. It's unearthly silent in there—no windows let in the sounds from outside, and it's far enough away that the noise in the hall doesn't reach it. It's like a tomb, buried at the heart of the school. Suspended.

He waits for the door to open. The nun comes out first, frowning at Avery as if he's not supposed to be here. Then Dan limps out. When Dan sees Avery, he adds a little more lag to his step. Then Erik, who doesn't even look up as he passes.

Finally Jacob. He flashes Avery his sunshine grin. "I've been thinking about you all day," he whispers. He bumps against Avery as if by accident. Avery feels the hardness coiled at Jacob's crotch when it presses briefly against Avery's butt. "We've got a lot of studying to do later."

He winks when he says that. Avery knows his books won't be opened tonight.

On the third day, the door is already open when Avery gets there. He hurries down the hall, his heart in his throat. All he can think is one of those boys said something else and there was another fight. No, he prays. Oh, God, no.

Inside the room, the nun sits behind her desk. She looks up as Avery enters. "Where...?"

"Monsignor's office," the nun tells him.

"They've decided?" Avery asks.

The nun looks at him for a moment, then nods. Before she can say another word, Avery runs out of the room and down the hall. At the monsignor's closed door, he stops. A moment later, he begins to pace. He'd give anything to hear what's going on in that office right now. Please let him stay here, he prays. Please don't let me lose him. Please.

When the monsignor's door finally opens, Avery rises to his feet. Jacob comes out scowling. He sees Avery but doesn't smile. "Well?" Avery ignores the other two boys and the nun who follows them out.

Jacob doesn't answer. Instead, he storms off down the hall. Avery catches up with him. "Jacob?" He wants to touch his arm, take his hand, but not with the others around. Lowering his voice, he adds, "What happened? Tell me what's wrong."

Jacob sighs, letting go of his anger. With a glance behind him to make sure the others aren't nearby, he asks, "Is there someplace we can go? Somewhere quiet?"

Avery feels his stomach knot inside of him. "Like where?" This can't be good.

Jacob shrugs. "The chapel?" he asks, hopeful.

"Choir rehearsal tonight," Avery says. "We can go to my room."

"What about Timmy?" Jacob wants to know.

Avery grins. "He's in the choir."

Avery's room is dark, just as he knew it would be. He clicks on the lamp by his bed, throwing shadows back into the corners.

Jacob takes off his blazer and begins to unbutton his shirt. Then he drops his books to the floor and sits on the edge of Avery's bed.

"Well?" Avery asks. He waits.

Jacob flops back on the bed. "I just keep telling myself it's not as bad as it could be."

Avery shrugs out of his own blazer and shirt. He shucks off his pants and kicks them away. In his T-shirt and boxers, he crawls onto the bed to lie down beside Jacob. He unbuttons his boyfriend's shirt the rest of the way, taking his time. Kissing Jacob's neck, he asks, "How bad could it be?"

"I could be kicked out." Jacob takes Avery's hand in his and eases it down until Avery cups his crotch. "How long will Timmy be gone?"

"Long enough." Avery unbuckles Jacob's belt and opens his zipper. "So you're not kicked out?"

Jacob shakes his head. When he turns, his mouth finds Avery's. Despite the sweet kiss, the press of tongue that slips between his lips, Avery pulls away. "Jacob," he warns. Beneath his kisses, Jacob moans. "You're not answering my question."

"I forget what it was," Jacob sighs. "Ask me again."

At Avery's stern look, Jacob smiles up at him. "I'm not expelled. I'm suspended for the rest of the semester, which isn't good. I can't fuck up again—"

"You're not expelled?" Avery lets out a sigh of relief and hugs Jacob close. He can't stop kissing him. He loves the taste of Jacob's skin, the feel of Jacob's flesh.

Between kisses, Jacob says, "I'm suspended, though. From now through winter break."

"We can handle that," Avery tells him. Suspension isn't too bad. At least they're still together. At least he's not expelled...

Beneath him Jacob gives in to Avery's kisses. His hands roam Avery's arms and chest, but something's wrong. Avery pulls back again to frown down at him. "Suspended?"

Jacob nods. His eyes are wide, fearful.

Avery feels his heart catch in his chest. "This isn't in-school suspension, is it?"

Slowly, Jacob shakes his head.

With a sigh, Avery rolls away from him. "Fuck."

"I have to be off school grounds by tomorrow night," Jacob whispers. He picks at Avery's nipple where it rises beneath his T-shirt. The sensation sends shivers down Avery's spine. "I've already called my mom. She's coming to get me tomorrow after mass."

Avery closes his eyes. How many more weeks do they have until the break? Two until Thanksgiving, another three past that. Then all of winter break, six weeks long. Jacob won't be back until classes resume. When is that? The second week of January and half a world away. "Tomorrow," he whispers.

Jacob nods again. He snuggles against Avery. His breath tickles Avery's neck, curling into the hollow of his throat. "Hold me, please?"

Avery slips his arms around Jacob, pulling his boy close. He's still thinking about the suspension. How many weeks is that? He isn't sure. "Jesus," he sighs.

"I'll be back next semester." Jacob kneads Avery's arm, fingers pressing into his flesh, his muscles. Fear fills his voice when he asks, "You won't forget about me before then, will you?"

Avery imagines the days ahead. Walking to mass, to class, to the library and the cafeteria, alone. How did he ever do it before he met Jacob? How will he do it now? "Tomorrow," he breathes again.

In his embrace, Jacob nods.

Avery blinks back sudden tears, promising himself he won't cry. "I'm going to miss you." His chin trembles. He hears his voice break.

Jacob buries his head in Avery's shoulder so aVERY won't see the tears shining in his eyes. "Do you want your ring back?" His voice is small, lost in Avery's shirt.

"No!" Avery cries. "God, no, Jacob. It'll just be a few weeks, that's all. You're still my boy. I still love you." He runs a hand through Jacob's curls. He loves the way they feel beneath his fingers, so soft, so impossibly soft. "I'll call you every night. I'll think about you every minute, I swear I will. And when I'm home for Thanksgiving, you can stay over my house, my mom won't mind. That's only what, two weeks away? If that. Two weekends. That's all, baby. We can make it that long."

"You really think so?" Jacob pulls away just enough to be able to look into Avery's face. He studies Avery's eyes as he brushes his fingertips across Avery's lips.

"We can make it." Avery kisses his fingers, then slips his hands beneath the waistband of Jacob's pants.

Jacob gasps at his touch. "If Timmy is going to be a while—"

"He won't be back before nine," Avery whispers into Jacob's neck. Jacob arches into him, pressing their bodies together with a sweet, painful crush. "Why?"

Jacob eases his hands beneath Avery's shirt and works it up Avery's chest. "Love me, then. Something to keep me warm until we do it again." He kisses down Avery's chest, his lips damp and hot and oh, so soft. "Thanksgiving?

Two weeks? God, can we wait that long?"

"I'll wait forever for you," Avery promises.

He's seventeen and in love, so he can say that. He knows it's true.

THE END

Without Sin

About the Author

J. Tomas is an author of gay YA romance who lives in Richmond, Virginia. More information and free short stories can be found online at http://www.j-tomas.net.

Without Sin

LaVergne, TN USA
26 January 2011
214074LV00004B/3/P